The Third Wave
& other Stories

The Third Wave
& other Stories

MILTON QUEAH

PARTRIDGE
A Penguin Random House Company

To order additional copies of this book, contact
Partridge India
000 800 10062 62
orders.india@partridgepublishing.com

www.partridgepublishing.com/india

DISCLAIMER

Dedicated to my dearest wife Manashi

CONTENTS

ACKNOWLEDGEMENT

I am immensely thankful to my entire family for their support and encouragement which has re-inspired me to take up writing yet once again after compelling circumstances had perforce driven me away from the wonderful world of ideas, thought and creativity. I am also greatly indebted to all my friends and well-wishers like the multitalented Dr Dinesh Baishya, the sharp shooter officer cop Rajen Singh, who had never lost their faith in me of being capable of writing, and especially to my demure friend Dhrubajyoti Hazarika, an established novelist and writer, and an accomplished bureaucrat, who could not restrain himself from ringing me up early one morning after reading one of my 'middles' in a local English daily, just to congratulate and encourage me, during those drab days.

My gratitude also goes to the entire Partridge family; Franco, Mark, Mary and others, and especially to Cleo who has been literally egging me on to complete my book, guiding me on ever so gently all the way.

My sincerest reverence goes out to that great silent body of individual human beings whose courage, determination and resolute struggle to overcome the challenges that come their way in the humdrum existence of everyday life have always been the prime source of inspiration of every writer down the ages.

THE BLACK GOAT

Not being descendants of some exclusive nobility or any landed aristocracy, my parents were generally averse to pets. They could hardly perceive that an exquisite sense of cultural refinement lay beneath this apparently perverted inclination to dote upon the lower animals. This attitude so naturally percolated through to the children that one would always find the younger ones running out with canes and sticks after any animal that unsuspectingly happened to roam anywhere near the precincts of the house. The older folk, though not so overtly militant as their juniors, were, nevertheless, strongly entrenched in their faith, being long initiated into the cult.

I very vividly remember an incident as a boy, when my sister and I brought home two very lovely kittens, twins they were. God! How much we had to plead and beg with the country girl to give them to us. The brown one was more infatuating, and I was particularly taken up by its color. Cats were either grey or black or black & white. Brown, as I knew then, was an exclusive dog color.

We came home jumping and dancing. But all our jubilations were shattered in an instant when Ma snatched the feline beauties from our laps and…!!! flung them across the courtyard, right into the kitchen garden. My sister started crying, but I was so startled that I stood stupefied, not one of my thousand simultaneous emotions being able to break through. The matter was solemnly reported to Dad when he came home from the office in the evening. He gave us a very patient hearing, but finally succeeded in satisfying us, by explaining at length how all cats were potential carriers of the TB germ, and the hazards which too close an intimacy with them entailed. This ultimately settled the matter, and Ma and we were friends once more.

We did not grow up to be positive animal haters. But our attitude towards them could hardly be called anything enthusiastic. We never had pets, nor did we ever feel any particular need of having one.

Things being always so, I was somewhat taken aback returning late home one evening to find the whole house in a flutter, just because some creature had unwittingly loitered into our drawing room. As soon as I stepped inside, I was dazzled by the sheer excitement everywhere. My sister (she was 19 now) tugged me by the sleeve, dragging me towards the room in the courtyard where we stored firewood. Having switched off the lights, she made me stand guessing in front of the closed door. The only answer that everyone gave to my impatient queries was "Just Guess, Just Guess". So I blurted out a long list of the most improbable things that ever could reside in a room where firewood and legs of broken tables are stored for years on end. But it was neither a Ridley tortoise nor a thick scaled pangolin. The thing that brushed against my legs as she majestically flung open the door was a darned black kid, with a belt round its neck. The whole family gloated over the big surprise they had given me, and I looked around in vain for someone to confide the singular misery I felt within for being taken to be so terribly surprised when I just simply wasn't. And so the celebration continued.

As night came on the general family mirth sobered down to a solemn decision-making deliberation; and after much lucubration, Dad finely opined: "Should anyone claim the lost goat, let it be returned forthwith. If not, let it stay, but only for so long as it pleases it to do so." My brother-in-law thought that it was a fugitive from the butchers' and was all for giving it asylum. But little Ena (my niece), who kept caressing it all throughout, was convinced that it was a wild goat from the neighbouring hills, which we could easily keep for ourselves. Babulal, our milkman, would tame it for us.

The morning, however, came as a boon to the sleepless night and it seemed to have solved our problems. The goat had wandered gracefully away while Ena was still asleep, and we were all immensely relieved.

The routine bathing, washing, cooking and polishing had almost taken the whole episode from our minds when Mrs Roy, our neighbor, came to return our iron. Sipping the hot cup of tea which Ma had offered her, she began to narrate how a hapless black goat had loitered into her house last evening and that she was planning to rear the hapless kid. At once we all rushed out and made a beeline for her house. And lo! There it was; the same black goat with the belt round its neck and the small white spot on its side, suspiciously tied near her kitchen. It was crystal clear that Mrs Roy had lied, and after some futile emotional outburst of protests and promises she finally gave in and confessed the truth. As the day wore on, the thing had become a matter of public concern now. The news spread from house to house like wild fire, and the whole neighbourhood was abuzz with conjectures and gossip; but the decision upon a suitable course of action had to be delayed, as all the male members of the locality were away in the offices.

That evening the children had no games. The men and women congregated at the local club and the goat was formally summoned there. The President asked for opinions.

Opinions similar to those put forward at our clandestine meeting the night before were repeated in drawling monotonous speeches almost ditto. Only little Ena, being firmly held down by her Mom, could not voice hers.

The important thing, it was realized after a considerable length of time, was not how it all happened, but what in the name of the Almighty, could now be done with it. Some suggested a general auction. Others were for a lottery. A few extremists from the back benches proposed a community picnic. But none of these could prevail over the ultimate socio-religious-cum-moral suggestion that it be let loose in the name of Ma Kamakhya (the revered local Deity), which would undoubtedly shower profuse blessings of the Goddess of Fertility upon the whole community.

Everyone connived, for opposition would be heresy. And so, the goat was profusely garlanded and let loose into the world, to roam and wander about unhindered and scot-free, until its very death.

*Sindur** was smeared on its forehead to immunize against the local butchers.

(Maligaon, Guwahati, October 1973)

THE ROAD ALONG
THE HILLSIDE

It must have been about five in the morning when I suddenly woke up. I slowly lifted the curtain and looked outside. An indescribably beautiful scenery greeted my bleary vision. The long grueling journey of the previous evening had thrashed the last bit of energy out of me, but now it was all well after a good night's sleep, and I was ready to take on another day of fresh adventure and experience of the countryside, which topped my agenda for the holidays.

A vast length of plain meadows stretched out in front of me running up to the foot of the hill at the far end. I picked up my binoculars and saw that the dark green hill slope was dotted with rows of tiny red-roofed houses, all so orderly lined. Each of the houses had a small garden in front, with pretty rose bushes, pergola of eglantine, massundas and finely arranged beds of assorted flowers. Quaint yellow wicket gates, dwarfed by cacti stood at the edge of well trimmed lawns of green. The plain was all vast and empty, except for a grove of mango trees which stood in a slouching huddle in the middle. The hill stood majestic covered by a film of mist which thinned away as it diffused across the vast plain, driven by the fresh morning breeze, enveloping everything with its translucent gossamer veil. The place was indeed beautiful. And as uncle had said, it did have a silent dignity of its own! A narrow road ran meandering along the base of the hill, throughout its entire length and disappearing beyond. But it was totally empty. No vehicle ever seemed to pass that way. It ran alone and silent along the hillside.

I was greatly taken up by the entire ambience and so pulled my pillow up and leaned against the window to have a closer look at the pristine vision which unfolded before my eyes. A girl dressed in a short white frock was plucking flowers in one of the gardens a few houses away from my uncle's plot. There was a peculiarity in the way she was plucking them. She plucked each flower sharply as a sting, but laid it in her basket, ever so tenderly, like a mother laying her newborn baby on the cot. I found it quite intriguing and so continued watching her for some time. A group of children were gathered under the mango grove. They were all gesticulating agitatedly and talking something among themselves, which I could not hear, looking up at the raw tempting mangoes which hung so high up. A few enterprising ones were throwing stones. But soon they gave up the effort in frustration and began to play different sorts of games as children of that tender age are wont.

The whole scene was simply enticing. The enchanted atmosphere was so very innocent and pure! The flowers, the grass, the red-roofed houses, the girl plucking flowers, the children playing around the mango grove and above all --- the hovering Mist, which spread its slow silent tentacles throughout, engulfing each and every object in its mighty sway! I turned my gaze and looked at uncle's garden just below my window. The bunch of red roses stared back at me with such a gaze of unabashed admiration that I blushed in embarrassment. The lush green lawn looked so very inviting. How wonderfully celestial it would be to lie down upon the soft dewy turf and sink in its bosom and sleep while the mist hovered over caressingly! I pressed my face against the grill to get a little more of the fresh breath of the morning breeze.....to get a little more of the raw dank smell of the green dewy grass...... a bit more of the delicate fragrance of the red blushing roses.....

Through a tiny gap in the thick mist which hovered above me, I suddenly spied a heavy blue truck come speeding up round a bend of the lonely road. It was moving at a reckless speed, and I could clearly hear the sound of the engine revving up, as it approached. I was all too familiar with the general wayward attitude of these highway drivers and the recklessness with which they drove whenever they found an empty road. I only prayed that nothing untoward would happen. Just as I was doing so, as hell would have it, the driver lost all control, and the truck skidded onto the grass and was running freely along the meadow, heading straight for the mango grove where the children were playing.

The girl plucking flowers saw it come and dropped her flower basket and ran for cover. But the children were still frolicking around the mango grove, laughing and shouting, oblivious of the catastrophe that was heading their way. I half sat up on the lawn where I lay and tried to shout, at the top of my voice, to warn them of the great impending danger, but all in vain. In spite of my best efforts, I could not utter a single monosyllable even. My voice was caught in my throat and I felt like choking in my own saliva! There was nothing I could do, but watch helplessly as the blue truck trundled heavily towards its deadly fate. I knew that the children would all be mowed down like stray puppies on the highway, in a matter of seconds! The fatal premonition sent shivers down my spine. My hairs stood on end and I was sweating profusely all over. As I looked on in utter consternation I saw the driver pop his head out and shout a warning at the children, waving his hand frantically, telling them to move out of the way. Shit! It was the very guy who had knocked down Satish and his bike last Friday when we were returning home after the cricket match at the varsity. But thank God, he somehow managed to divert the speeding truck this time round and avoid hitting the mango grove directly. But in doing so, he had veered around viciously and was now speeding head on towards my direction. To the very place where I lay!

The sense of immediate impending bodily harm made me forget everything else and I was bothered about nothing but my own survival. I turned over to escape and run. But much as I tried I could not move an inch! My hands went limp and my legs were held firmly to the ground by some overwhelmingly overriding invisible power. I knew that I had been bewitched. The mist and the grass had cast their mysterious spell on me! I rued my impudence, and wished I had never expressed my weakness for them so openly. I was now totally in their thrall! The truck would simply run me over and kill me. My eyes popped in their sockets as I beheld the monstrous truck come head on. The headlights… the bumper…the radiator grid…the black lethal grooved rubber wheels!

The replay of the last nineteen years of my young life flashed through my mind in a nano second! Oh No! No! Stop! Stop! Stop! I shut my eyes in utter desperation, awaiting the final crunch…. But nothing happened! There was an eerie inexplicable silence all around…. Was I dead or alive? The truck had stopped inches away from me. I knew it, but didn't dare to look.

Slowly I opened my eyes and tried to take a peep. Through the slits of my eyelashes I could vaguely discern the ubiquitous blue colour of the truck, as it straddled over me, like a mighty colossus. My pride and smugness sank within me and I painfully came to realize my true worth. The degrees that I had acquired, the talents that I flaunted, all those clever ideas in my head, all those topics of fiery debate on nationalistic jingoism and world vision didn't mean a thing to me any longer. Everything had vanished before my abject physical vulnerability. Being incapable of defending myself against a mere wayward truck!

I opened my eyes wider. I could still see the blue colour, but there was no sign of any truck around. How foolish of me, I thought. Of course, there was no truck! How could there be? I must be looking at the blue open sky from the lawn where I lay…. I rubbed my eyes harder and looked up in surprise. Damn it! It was the blue newly painted ceiling I was staring at!

I jumped out of my bed where I had dozed off and looked out the window again. The vast undulating plain ran its full stretch right up to the hill which loomed majestically in the distance, dotted with the neat rows of red roofed houses with pretty lawns and rose-bushes in front of them. The mango grove too stood there, as it was, in the middle of the meadow, in that same slouching huddle, but there were no children playing beneath it, any longer. The flower girl too had gone. And the road?... There it was! …meandering along the base of the hill, throughout its entire length and beyond. But it was still as empty as ever. No vehicle ever seemed to pass that way. It ran alone and silent along the hillside.

(Gauhati University 1975)

THE BOSS

It's a damned hell of a place where I work. It's real sad that I landed up here. God alone knows how long I'd be able to survive here. This certainly is no place for people of decent tastes and habits. The dilapidated rented building, the dirty narrow staircase and the foul stinking toilets! The whole ambience is one of utter confusion, with heaps of files dumped haphazardly and rolls of waste paper littered all over the place. Even the clients who come to the office are equally insensitive. They spit on the staircase landings covering the walls with the brown stains of chewed betel juice at will. With blackened cobwebs dangling from the ceilings, the place resembles more a backstreet slum than a business agency office. It is not only the attitude of the visitors but that of the staff as well, who are equally callous, which has helped to turn the place into a veritable bedlam. They spend most of their time indulging in idle talk and cracking jokes that verge more on the lewd than being anything funny. This sundry gossip and malicious slander is laced up by vigorous rubbing of tobacco and lime on their palms, while endless cups of horrible tasting tea do the rounds along with platters of *tamul-pan* generously spread out among the bundles of challans, drafts and invoices. The tables and chairs are all dotted with white stains of insensitively rubbed lime.

Unlike banks or corporate offices, where you find a certain sort of uniformity of appearance among the staff, here there is a conglomeration of prototypes. The leading ones are those with flushed faces, fat oozing from their cheeks bearing eloquent testimony to their intemperate lifestyle. Their breaths reek of stale liquor and undigested food. These though boisterous by nature, are generally harmless. The counterpoint is provided by the lean types, who are so shrunk that the belt around their emaciated waist lines, buckled up to the very last hole, acts more like a rope to keep the trousers in place. Their shirts hang loose upon their lean shoulders, as that of a scarecrow. But these are the real deadly types. Their morose deadpan faces conceal a brain which is a repository of the deadliest venom, and who are capable of killing any initiative with a single lash of their lethal tongue. Peering over their thick-rimmed glasses they can identify a file from a distance by the mere look of its cover. These are the ones who have mastered the art of hiding important files and misplacing vital documents at will, compelling the toughest of clients to go round and round until they come back, begging on their knees, with offer of un-resented bribe.

The women staff are a class apart. They are full of information --- a veritable cornucopia of malicious gossip. They seem to know about the private lives of everyone of note around town, and are capable of giving vivid descriptions of the secret lives of individuals, as if they had been present in their very bedrooms, catching them in the actual act. The office, for them, is a forum for exchanging the knowledge of recipes and updating the latest offers at shopping malls and rebate data. This is the general state of affairs which I have to contend with everyday. Just imagine all your colleagues coming to office at their own sweet will, their filthy mouths full of the foulest of curses, often exhaling fumes of stale liquor! At times, it is a real mortification to hear one of these morons ranting about his night-long escapade with some formidable trull or of some such other banality. Alas! I had to take up this job which came first my way. Economic compulsions, that's it! I had to even leave my postgraduate studies half way. All day I sit here and listen to these wasters ranting their heads away. And then there is the steno-typist girl, the rich plum on the cake --- a downright seasoned bitch! An Amazon type with a beleaguered look, whose native beauty had turned grotesque from over-usage and early indiscretion! She's the Personal Secretary to our Boss and looks after all his needs, even the emotional ones, they say. Not even the maintenance boy, I am told, ever forgoes the chance to plant on her a kiss.

This, however, isn't all. There is yet another personality, a star that outshines every other. It's the Boss. He is an outright bully, a sort of *dada*. He fumes and frets and scowls over every small issue, and often hits out in ferocious rage. He's a veritable terror! Everyone falls mute when he enters, being well acquainted with his enterprising manners. But I care two hoots for him and have a total contemptuous disregard for whatever he says or does. That's what the like of him deserve. Damned bull that he is!

It's been just over six months since I joined here. But even within this short spell, I have been witness to one full-fledged fight and three or four other minor scuffles. Two guys have already been suspended. On one such occasion even the police had to be called in, to bring things under control. This queer sort of melodrama goes on intermittently, and every three months, on an average, there is either a head broken, a hand injured, a nose flattened etc. But what is most surprising is that no one has ever tried to put an end to all this. No one ever dares to protest against this outrageously rude behavior of the Boss. These guys, I tell you, are real knaves; a cluster of duds accustomed to bow and bend all their lives. What can one expect of them? Had it been me… Upon my word! I would have taught him such a good lesson that he would have remembered it for the rest of his life. The Dirty Skunk!

But, frankly speaking, so far I haven't had any trouble with the Boss. Whenever he looks at me, I look him back straight in the face. He just says nothing, nor do I. Regarding the work too, there's been no complaint so far. And why should there be? I complete most of the work regularly. What else can I do? The work is the only decent thing that one can do around here. But I'm prepared to meet all eventualities, anyway. I'm neither a coward nor a knave. God! I'd die if someone would ever think me that! After all, what can the Boss do to me? Scold me…wrongly? I'll make him eat his words. Would he hit me? I'll batter his brains out; if he ever tries to (I always keep the thick metal ruler handy). I'll show him someday…. That Wild Boar!

The Boss usually lands up around two in the afternoon, and everyone makes it a point to return to their desks well before that. Once he is there, no more of idle talks or going out for cups of tea. Believe it or not, some think twice even to go for a pee… Oh hell! Its 1:35 already, the Boss would be there anytime now! I had been totally unaware how time had flown by. The lunch break was over. There was no time to go for a quick snack even! ….But what was there to get so worked up about? I'm only going for a cup of tea! I slowly got up from my seat and just walked out of the office, slamming the main door after me.

Out in the street it was hell hot. I coolly lighted a fag and crossed over to the restaurant across the street. It was fully crowded. Somehow I managed to find a seat in the corner. "One chicken roll and a Pepsi! Real cold…" I barely managed to place my order with the waiter who rushed passed me through the crowd of customers and vanished behind the counter, abandoning me to an anxious wait for some fifteen minutes or so. It was getting real late now! I lighted up another cigarette to ease the tension. There was still no sign of him! I was just about to scream, when he suddenly appeared and put the roll and the lukewarm soft drink in front of me. "There's been no power since morning Sir", he explained, before I could speak. The next eating joint was some hundred meters down the street....there's no time to go there. The Boss would be there at the office any moment now! No..... It's not him though....its damned too hot to walk the distance...Yep! That's it!

I settled down cozily in my seat, took a bite of the roll and began sipping the lukewarm drink while my eyes wandered lazily along the street; among the traffic and the crowd of people hurrying by. I could clearly see the main entrance of the office from where I sat. The gates were still closed. The Boss hadn't come as yet... Just then a car zoomed past and came to a screeching halt behind two ladies, loaded with shopping, forcing them to scurry on to the foot path. I suddenly noticed the embossed number plate of the vehicle: ASZ 5258. Hell! It's the Boss! I must hurry.... No! Why should I? I'm not doing anything wrong! Just having a bite, that's it. What's there to be so shit scared about? I'm not a knave? Let me take my time. So I kept sitting...sipping leisurely...tastily...

It was exactly twenty past two when I entered the office. Everyone was staring at me as if I had won some gladrags contest or something. I just looked away and went to my seat and sat down slowly, with as much composure as I could muster. "Boss has come", Prakash whispered. 'So what?' I didn't bother to look up. "He enquired about you". 'So what?'

"He was a little…" Before Prakash could finish the office peon came up to me and said that the Boss wanted to see me right away. My heart gave a suppressed leap. I got up, looked around and (with a great deal of effort to keep calm) walked towards the imposing plywood chamber. "Come in!" the Boss roared, even as I turned the knob. I entered with my head slightly bowed. "Where'd you been Youngman?" the roaring went on. "I'd…I'd just gone for a cup of tea Sir". "How's that?", the roar sobered into a quizzical grin. "Do you need an hour and a half to have your tea?" His lips spread in a sneering smile. "You have a full hour's break for lunch. Don't you? What's that extra half an hour for? What nonsense is this? I don't know how you can account for it! I had clearly made it known to you when you had joined, that sincerity and punctuality is all I demand. Besides, I had already announced that I wanted all the pending loan files cleared by 3:30 pm, as I have an urgent meeting with the bank at 4 O'clock today. I want all the account statements ready and in order before that. What about those stack of files lying on your table? Is this the sort of responsibility you have? I just don't know what might be the meaning of such knavish behavior".

A wild tremor ran through me. Knave…? Could he dare call me a knave? My knees throbbed, my head went dizzy and the ground began to move beneath my feet, as if. I clutched the table so tight that my knuckles showed white. I can't possibly take this insult lying down…and that too from an insolent pig! My face flushed red and I was sweating all over. I wanted to scream, to burst out and shout and tear him to pieces. But only my lips quivered. There was a lump stuck in my throat. I couldn't speak a word! My mouth went dry and I felt like choking. My arms went totally limp. God! I was suffocating! "I haven't started a charity home here", he went on attacking, down and defenseless as I was, his words reaching me in a haze.

"I can't afford to keep parasites on my wage roll", the roaring went on. "If such irresponsible behavior is repeated in future, I'll have no other option but to strike you off the rolls. That's that! Do you follow? Now go! Finish those files. There's hardly some thirty minutes left before I leave. I doubt you'll be able to finish them all. Anyway go!" "Yes Sir", I lisped and turned heavily for the door. "Wait a moment", he called after me. I stopped, and turned passively to take some more beating. There was no feeling left in me, whatsoever. "Our Company's subsidiary is having their AGM sometime in the third week of next month, although they haven't fixed the exact date as yet." His words reached me from a distance, as if. "Most probably, I might not be able to attend due to clash of dates with the Board meeting. I was thinking of sending someone else instead. What if we send you? Will you be able? You see, I want someone who would be able to make a fair presentation of the achievements of our unit, there at Bombay. What say you? Is it OK?" I was utterly stupefied and stood speechless. Somehow I managed to lisp "Yes Sir", and rushed back to my seat to clear those pending files.

(Maligaon, Guwahati, 1977)

YAHOO

Dust flew up madly and entered the eyes and nostrils as the empty truck swerved sharply from the main road and trundled onto the rough graveled mud track with a huge jolting thud. Clouds of dust rose up like red smoke, and went dancing behind it, in a weird chiaroscuro of orange and grey, as it sped headlong towards the sunset, which lay straight ahead. Yahoo squinted repeatedly, as was his habit, and cursed under his breath. Had he not moved fast enough, with the heavy load on his back, he would have been knocked over, for sure. These truck drivers were real bastards! They acted in such a way, as if, the road was their father's property, and they owned it all. In suddenly trying to rush out of the way, Yahoo had strained his neck and pulled a nerve, from the effort. But there was no high ground anywhere nearby, where he could not put down the heavy load, which was on his back, strapped firmly to his forehead. He had no other option but to bear the searing pain, and trudge along the dusty trail until he crossed the farm gate and reached the foot of the hills beyond.

The 5 O'clock shuttle was hooting past at a distance, and hearing it, he knew, that he had rightly decided on not taking the short cut, which ran through the railway colony, instead of this longer route through the *Gaushala*, the sacred cattle farm. The children would all be out on the colony street, by now, and would have made his life a hell again, had he gone that way. He shuddered at the thought and the trauma of it all. That's why he best avoided the colony road, although it was much shorter, unless it was absolutely necessary or there was some hurry. For some unknown reason, these colony children were always after his blood. And it wasn't something new; but a tradition of sorts, which had been passed on down the generations, as if. It had started with the older boys some of whom had now become fathers. Now their children were keeping the ritual alive. No sooner they sighted his stocky figure approaching from a distance, they would go berserk, as if, and run towards him and surround him with ear-splitting yells of "Yaaho…Yahoo….Yaaaahoo".

Much as he tried, no matter what methods he employed, he just could not shake them off his trail. They would soon be joined by others, all shouting and yelling in a riotous chorus, as unruly brats are wont, whenever they saw a mad man or some mad dog. Yahoo (nobody ever knew his real name) too, in his turn, would shout back at them; pouting the filthiest of expletives, generously supplemented with an array of lewd gestures and exhibitionistic peek-a-boo nudism. The children would get further excited by this and go wacky. The free road show would go on, every meter of the two hundred meter stretch of the colony road, and would come to an end only with his descent onto the *kutcha* hillside path beyond, which cut off the line of vision, at the bend.

Although it was quite unclear, how he had come to inherit this unusually exotic Swiftian sobriquet, anyone who saw him once, could hardly deny its appropriateness. Short and stocky, with a crop of brownish spiky matted hair, dark rounded cheeks, and a pair of permanently squinting eyes, sporting an off-white T-shirt two measures undersize and a pair of khaki shorts clinging to his stolid waist on a string and a prayer, he was quite a caricature to look at. The pair of shorts, plagued with holes and patches all over, were tucked away at so very many impossible angles that it served more in highlighting those parts, than which it was supposed to conceal.

The strap of the heavy sack which he was carrying on his back, was straining against Yahoo's sweating forehead, and he was feeling very thirsty, in the sweltering late afternoon heat. He looked around for some raised ground to lay down the load and take some rest. Finding none on the long reddish mud track, he decided to slog it on for some time more, until he came to the foot of the hill where a stream meandered down among the huge shady rocks. The spot lay mostly isolated at this hour, except for some late women bathers. It was like a base camp for Yahoo; where he would often put off his load, and have a wash and refresh himself, before embarking on the steep climb to the villages uphill. The hills were as old as the people who lived in them; consisting mostly of the native Bodo and Garo tribes of Assam. The Nepali settlements, wherein he stayed, were relatively new, consisting of immigrants who had come and settled over the years. The general proclivity for use of khaki clothes by the men, especially the older ones, suggested that they had, at some time or the other, served in the armed forces, or as security guards or watchmen. But most them had now reverted to their traditional business back home, of rearing cows and selling milk. It was mostly this group of people, who were Yahoo's paymasters. His job lay in carrying the sack-loads of fodder bought in the market below and delivering them to their arduous destinations up the hill.

It was almost dark by the time he reached the stream. Putting down the enormous load off his back onto a smooth rock, Yahoo stepped into the clear stream, and splashed his face and head vigorously with the cold water to take the heat off. He did not know how long he must have been at it. Finally, soaked and dripping all over, he clambered out of the water and slumped onto a big flat rock, in total exhaustion.

The shrill call of the crickets and the buzzing sound of insects, humming around his face, woke him up. He hadn't realized when he had dozed off. He must have been asleep on the rock there for almost an hour or so, for it was dark all around. He squinted vigorously cursing under his breath, and rose up in haste to go. As he was fitting the sling-strap around his forehead and was about to raise the load onto his back, he glanced at the field below and stood aghast. A long beam of glimmering light lay suspended in mid-air right across the field in front of him. A thick row of myriad fireflies were floating in the air, carrying their translucent greenish-yellow lanterns of light, stretching far away into the distant darkness.

The glittering chain of light swayed and scattered with the movement of the breeze, forming bizarre aerial motifs, on the necklace of some demon princess, as if. Yahoo was overwhelmed by a strange emotion he did not know how to express. He merely stood there gasping; his chinky eyes squinting, more rapidly than ever before, in the dark. No Wordsworth to draw any analogy of the vision, with the Milky Way, Yahoo indifferently turned to leave with his heavy load, which suddenly seemed to feel light compared to the burden which hung heavy on his untutored heart. It was here, among these very rocks, where they used to sit together and laugh; he and Manu, his sweetheart.

She was very young then, and very playful and full of life. How she used to splash the water on him and run away, jumping from one rock to the other, like some nimble –footed mountain goat. How he used to lumber clumsily after her, panting and sweating, and finally slump onto her fragile lap, and continue lying there as if in paradise, while she mopped the sweat off his forehead, caressing him like a child! He was willing to give away everything for her; his very life, if need be. How excited she was, when he had bought her that set of colorful glass bangles during the annual *Gaushala* cattle fair two years ago! She had insisted that he should himself put them onto her wrists. She was looking so gorgeous, even in the dark, her red *ghagra* skirt and *choli* blouse glittering in the floodlit moonlight. He had also bought some fresh sugar cane for her that day. How she had sat beside him on the rock, her slim fair legs kicking the water playfully, as she peeled off the bark with her white shining teeth, chewing the cane and talking all the while. How tender and warm was the feel of her cheeks, against his rough stubble! How fragrant the youthful aroma of her presence! How so very mellifluous and sweet was Life! How so much sweeter than the sugarcane!

The ghostly beam of light was no longer visible, nor was the field. He had winded his way far uphill. The thick bamboo groves swayed heavily in the night wind, making a creaky haunted sound. They hardly allowed any light to filter through, and so Yahoo had to carefully watch his steps while moving on the uneven ground. The spirits, they say, will sometimes lay a lone bamboo across your path; and one had to be wary enough to detect it, well in time, and avoid stepping over it. If anyone happened to step over by mistake, the fallen bamboo would suddenly rise erect and throw him high up in the air, whence from he would fall and smash his skull against the ground, and die a most horrendous death. He wickedly wished that some such sort of thing would happen to that driver, Bir Bahadur, who had snatched his beloved Manu from him.

He peeped through the grove and could see the flickering hurricane light behind the split-bamboo walls of Manus's house. The bastard must be inside there, drinking with Manu and her mother. The mother was a bitch and a very heartless woman…Look, how cunning she was! All these years she used to be so very sweet to him. She knew very well how much he loved Manu, and so took advantage of him. Manu and he had grown up together from childhood, had played together, and were almost inseparable. She knew it all. Why else, would she have asked him to accompany her, wherever she went? She had, it seemed, entrusted her only daughter to his care. She had expressly asked him to look after her and to protect her always. And he had ungrudgingly accepted the role. He had been doing all the sundry jobs of the household for them over the years; fed and watered the cattle, gathered jungle wood, split the logs for firewood, milked the cows… and all this for free. Why? Because he had considered them his own! A part of his family!

Then, why did she now suddenly turn her back upon him, treating him like a total stranger? Keeping him in the dark and giving away Manu in marriage to someone else who had done nothing for her! Was there nothing called Trust in this world? Was there nothing called Love? He had half a mind to barge in, and give them all a piece of his mind and a good thrashing, to take off the heavy burden which was breaking his heart. But he bit his lips hard and restrained himself. Painful tears of deep felt hurt oozed out of his bleary eyes, below the sling-strap straining against his bursting forehead. He quickly gathered himself up, squinted rapidly and went along.

As the giant bamboo groves continued to rustle ominously in the strong night wind, Yahoo trudged his weary way forward, along the lonely forest path, disappearing round the next thick bamboo grove, carrying his heavy load with him. His dull-witted brain could not comprehend the complex ways of the world. The childlike simple questions of his heart would never find an answer. For how, in all the world, would he be able to ever know or comprehend the weird logic behind the decision of Manu's mother, who had set it as a secret precondition for the lecherous driver, that if he wanted to be her lover, he would have to marry her daughter; in order to protect her from the ravages of a rapacious world that thrives on feeding upon the predicament of indigence and sheer poverty.

(Maligaon, Guwahati, 1979)

TO MOVIES JUST

The Youngman hurrying through the noisy traffic was a sexual pervert. Not that his looks and appearance gave him away though. Dressed impeccably in a pair of plain formal trousers and a full sleeved shirt, well tucked in and buttoned up to the wrist, he looked every inch a thoroughbred gentleman that any civilized society would be proud of. He stopped to light a fag, although there was no particular need for one. He just thought it OK to inhale a few puffs of the dusty smog as the twilight was setting in. He walked fast, and with a bouncy gait, as if he had some appointment to keep or may be to meet someone who was waiting for him ---some girl, sweetheart, lover or what the hell they called it, he did not know.

Abir was going for a movie, but no girl awaited him there. He wasn't one of those suckers who spent money on vagrant girls. After all, why should he? Was it his enjoyment alone? Didn't they satisfy their longing desire and hollowness; their arid starvation and lust, when they came to him? Why then should he, like a sop, pay for it alone? But the question of money, however, was not that important. What really bothered him a goddamned hell was not money but Wooing; an art which he had never learnt all these years, and perhaps never would all his life. He just couldn't relish the idea of running after someone, trying to win her favour, persuading her to condescend to satisfy her own lust upon him. Often he would laugh; laugh aloud at the ridiculously programmed exactitude with which all this game of love-making was being played. What methods! He wondered. What madness!

The blank stares of half sex-starved girls, dressed in their dazzling finery, rushing out on the very first celebration that came their way; hopeful of being noticed, and those ranting young boys, moving in herds in front of girls' hostels, passing remarks that only hit the bare walls, made his heart ache and feverish. He wanted to do away with it all. What need was there was for such a society which made slaves of men and women alike? Dumb castrated creatures who could not give vent to their strongest natural physical passion; thus left to degenerate into inveterate social perverts!

It was 5:15 pm, and he had ten minutes still. It would take five minutes, at the most, if he hurried. In fact, it would not matter even if he reached a little late. After all, they would be showing all those stupid commercials for the first half an hour or so. In fact it would not even matter even if he went in after the Interval, as all Hindi movies usually got into business only in the second half. The first half was all crap, with boisterous jokes and flower-park romancing where the songs were as long winded as the heroine's color-changing saris.

Today he was again in that sub-normal mood. His mind was all blank except for a stray thought that he might find a seat beside a nice cute girl or some young unescorted lady. That would be enough to while away the time meaningfully in the theatre hall. He could not bear the thought of being nestled between two sweating hulks for those long two hours or so.

The last time he had sat beside a woman in a movie hall was long back, when he had gone with Vandana to watch that off-beat film. It was an insipid big farce. And he had laughed at the film, at her and at himself. She was yet another of those pseudo ultra-modern girls whom, by now he had come to know too well. So forward and stinging with the tongue, but down in the ditch where true sexual relationships were concerned. She had sat taught in her seat, not even letting her bare slender shoulders to casually brush his. She said she disliked the sexual scenes. And he had laughed …laughed aloud. What naïve pretensions! He could clearly discern the lingering starvation in her eyes; on her lips. Here was yet another martyr of our time-honoured morality and modesty! He mused. But how could anyone help her if she herself deliberately wanted to remain in shackles? It was indeed a pity; an infinitely ironic pity! Because all the time she had been thinking herself to be modern, sophisticated---liberated.

What an act she had put on that afternoon! He was caught all unawares when she had called out to him from behind in the long corridor leading to the lecture halls, when he was on way to the class. She wanted to go for a movie, she said; but wondered how she would go all alone. He had asked her to cut all that crap and say plainly whether she wanted him to accompany her or not. She bubbled that it would be great, and had excitedly gone back to the hostel to change and get ready requesting him to wait for her at the Varsity bus stand. She would be there in twenty minutes sharp. But she had failed to show up even after waiting an hour. Being downright fed up with all this Reformationistic coquetry he had left her and gone ahead alone, leaving her to follow if she ever wanted to.

The crowd outside the hall was huge. He was badly short of cash, but waiting for her to come would make no sense, as all the tickets would have been sold out by then. So he had plunged headlong into the crowd and literally fought his way through to the counter and managed to pluck the two tickets out, almost like the Golden Fleece, hurting his left arm badly in the process. As he stood sweating and nursing his injured hand, there she was! Standing and smiling in her tight jeans and short printed top, apologizing for being late. She had also suddenly got concerned about his arm. But he had just looked at her and said "Let's go in, the picture is about to begin."

5:25 pm. He had reached the hall just in time. "One Balcony", he said, thrusting his hand through the counter. He earnestly hoped to get a seat beside some classy woman who had a mature and wholesome notion of sex. Older women always attracted him more than those tom-boyish embodiments who knew little else besides jumping in and out of their thirty odd jeans and munching on fried popcorns.

The seat he got was in the middle, left of the aisle, in the second row from the bottom. A couple was sitting next on his right. But even before he could sit down, they had already inter-changed places, the man interposed as a safe buffer between him and the lady. He dimly guessed it was all over, although two seats still lay vacant to his left. The lights had now started dimming. People were still coming in one after the other. He watched them anxiously go by like the numbers on the Wheel of Fortune, waiting for the one who would ultimately hit the empty chair next to him.

The lights went on dimming further, and with them his hopes, when a thick corpulent hulk of a gentleman entered and clambered onto the empty seat next to him. The inevitable had happened. The fatso pulled a perfumed hanky from his pocket and wiping the profuse sweat off his balding forehead sank his ample bottom into the seat giving forth a stinking sigh of relief, innocent of the dire pang his presence had caused to the man beside him. After this, it was all men and men. Streaming in, in all shapes and sizes; as they come. Coming in painful succession…hopeful, thoughtful, expectant and anxious. Hollow men groping haplessly for their stuffed seats in the dark.

The door opened ominously yet once again. Abir sprang upright in his seat. Two ladies, looking magnificent in the confused lights, stood for a moment in the doorway, in a stunning silhouette of oriental lure. Led by the usher, they coquettishly high-heeled their way, rustling gracefully through the rows of chairs and knees, to the empty seats right in front of him, in the half empty row just below. They gracefully settled their saris and sat down in their seats sending forth wafts of sensual perfume all around.

Nearly a full reel must have been shown when Abir became aware of it all. He looked at the screen and then tentatively at the row below, and all around him. A strong feeling propelled him, egging him on, to change seats. But he did not move. Time and again it came. But he shrank. The roaring laughter all around brought him to with a start. He collected his thoughts and sat upright. What were they all laughing at? He instinctively gathered himself up in defence. No! They hadn't guessed what he was up to. Damn! How could they? How stupid of him to think so! It was perhaps one of those lusty cheers they gave the hero, who realized their mortified desires on the screen. The ladies too laughed. But were they genuine? He couldn't be sure. By now his eyes had become quite used to the dark, and he could see them clearly. One of them, he thought, came quite up to the mark. She knew how to dress in that formidable blend of show-a-little, hide-a-little, which the docile Indian sari is so capable of. Yes! It could indeed sometimes become a lethal weapon in the hands of an Indian serpent of the Nile.

But the question, nevertheless, remained. Whether her wiles stopped at her dress, or went beyond? She did not look that naïve. Perhaps they did.

The Intermission came glaring on with lights; unweaving all those intricate webs of fantasy spun in lonely quietude and the dark. Darned blasted Lights! They were menacing…. But they too had their charm once; much before he had even known Ruby, his first college flame. A strange mania had seized him then, and he lived in a world of flamboyance and glamorous glitter. It was all show and exhibition. And there used to be quite a kick in it too. Even a particular color of the button had its draw, not to speak of dog-collars and leather patches on faded denims. It was a time when Daylight was a Delight. There could not have been enough of it. It was always Light, more Light and more. The night was a sad thing then --- a time to return home; to loneliness, to frustration and to your empty bed. How lonely it had all seemed! Alone among the whole family! Loneliness was too much for him. He could not bear it. He had to run away to parties, to picnics, to get-togethers; to crowds where boys and girls could meet … mix freely.

But now darkness was the only recourse; the only solace and refuge. He didn't dare to venture out into the staring daylight. How confusedly it made a mess of him! His dress, his hair and steps would all be in one grand disconcert…so many arms, so many legs. But the night was a time of respite, of comfort and of self-confidence, when he could walk with a proud gait and a bold heart, because there was none to see, no one to take notice. Thank heavens! The lights had started dimming into a soothing darkness once more, turning the entire hall into a detached, nameless silhouetted audience. The ladies too were there…faceless.

The end was looming large and everything was moving fast towards it. The loose ends were hurriedly being tied up, perforce, as it were. It did not matter how one did it. The important thing was to end it somehow. The symptoms of the end were banal --- A false climax, followed by yet another. A sham chase, fast action and fight, with quite a number of shots repeated generously, all ending with the inevitable arrival of so many people in uniforms. It was always the same old tedious stuff. He knew it all too well to try and defend his foolish indulgence, by talking of art, cinematography or of just killing time. If there was anything at all, it was the sexy screen that held some explanation. To look for any other insipid interpretations would be downright asinine. Or was it one of those listless ramblings for contact with women that had brought him here today? He couldn't be quite too sure; although it couldn't be just wished away either. Women held such a peculiar place in his life which he could neither define nor explain. His sporadic attempts to understand it had landed him nowhere. Sometimes he realized, how unnecessary it was to love or be loved. What magical charm or power there was in the thing called Love which made a man or woman so devotedly yoked to each other, so as to sacrifice anything and everything, even at times, their very lives, he could never comprehend. He only knew that he was an entity. A living creature that had to eat, drink and keep alive till death. What did other things actually matter? The gaping void of Life was too great for some single woman or man or many, for that matter, to fill. Was there anything that could ever fill it? Was there any particular need for filling it at all? If there was anything that came anywhere near to doing that, it was Religion. But conviction played havoc with idyllic religious tenets in the face of the harsh realities of life. Sometimes he prayed, and often his prayers were answered.

But he was at a loss to explain why he could not somehow believe in any tenet in full. People said he was pig-headed, paradoxical, living in a dream world, and all that. How he wished that the business of living could be put down in some neat formulae. Something which could be proved, codified, defined and predicted.

He admired the dedicated life of the ancient sages; their austere lifestyle of devotion and silent meditation. But they were no longer to be seen these days. He had, perhaps been born a little too late to enable them to extricate him from this quagmire of chaos and non-entity where to seek for meaning seemed to be a heresy. Perhaps the world had come round a full circle. Perhaps we were entering a New Age of Belief. But the spiraling had not been upwards. From blind faith in God, we have traversed to a condition, where we are compelled to profess a blind faith in Nothingness and Meaninglessness which is beyond nihilism, where the Mighty God, the space scientists were looking for, might turn out to be a mass of some mere chemical gas or magnetic force with auto intelligence. No! The prophets were all too very wrong. They did not open up a vista of knowledge of the Unknown. All they did was to impose their self-realizations upon the gullible millions, who had neither the time nor the ability to think for themselves. Following their prescriptions would not do. We were all, each one of us, our own prophets, be it prophets of tom-foolery or prophets of doom.

How tragic it all was! Not to be allowed the understanding of one's most insignificant of deeds; one's silliest actions! It was always a blank, a very big zero and always the same. He just couldn't know why he had been doing them; even as he could not find a reason as to why he had come for the movie so hurriedly today. What did he expect? Pleasure..? Joy? What would he do with happiness?

Would it make any difference? All sorts of questions began to riddle his mind. Oh! It was all so very maddening! He needs must give up. The only solid reason that he could think of, as he lighted a fag outside the hall, was that it was nothing but an outlet for the ever craving desire of his very being, for women --- for girls. This was the only plausible fact, which he did not have to garnish or upholster. It was the only fact, in the acknowledgement of which he did not have to bluff himself. It was the sole truth about him, in its purest essence. All the rest were trinkets, masks, fancy locks, knives and decorative key chains which he carried about him, like some hapless railway platform vendor. In acknowledging that, he was himself. He felt fulfilled. He felt like being Real ---he felt his very Existence. Like other animals and living and non-living things, he was one with the Universe. He could joyfully fit himself into a formula; but sadly, only to an extent. How often he wished he had no other business in life but to look for fresh grass, unhindered among a flock! How much easier would it have been to find that elusive fulfillment, for which his soul craved, in that idyllic condition.

Of all living things, it was the Tree, perhaps, which he considered to embody the highest form of Life. Standing silent and unassumingly out there in the open air, roughing all weather, it showered a cornucopia of blessings on everyone and everything around, keeping nothing for itself. Without having to frantically move about or hunt, it provided its own nourishment from the very soil upon which it stood, soaking in the light from the sun and water from the clouds. It sustained life by releasing life-giving oxygen for the benefit of all and drawing in the toxic carbon dioxide to itself, even like Lord Shiva who drank the poison himself, to save humankind. Giving its leaves and branches for shade and shelter; fruits, flowers, nuts and berries for food; the bark, roots and sap for medicine and chemicals, and finally its very life-wood for building houses, boats and ships, furniture for the home and fuel for the hearth and factory and ending up by providing firewood for the ultimate funeral pyre... And all this for free! If this utter selflessness be not Divine Providence, then what is? If this absolute self sacrifice be not Divine Love, then what is? If this unobtrusive detachment be not Divine Nirvana, then what is?

In spite of his numerous emotional orgies, he had never really experienced the depth of a woman's love, and wondered if there was anything like it at all. Could anyone love him in a more different way than how Ruby, Vandana, June or Nilufer & Co. had done? Was there anything called pure love? Or was it one of those hallucinatory trances which an un-heroined mind is susceptible to?

He hated himself for not being able to enjoy what everyone else enjoyed. He was no hermit or some sky-clad *digamber*; poignantly disdainful of the evanescent pleasures of this illusory world. No, he wasn't like that at all! He too wanted to partake in pleasures; he too wanted to enjoy. But the tragedy was that, he could not satisfy himself that the things which people generally enjoyed, were really capable of being enjoyed so much as they were made out to be. To him, these could, at best, only bring about a change of mood. Indeed they could; but that too only ephemerally and in a state of unthinking. For thought was our bane. It would never allow us to go illogical or insane, and so prevent us from being really happy. For happiness is inseparably linked to a state of suspended sanity. Perhaps there could never be a reason for enjoyment, but only a reason for enacting an enjoyment scene at some moments in our lives. He recalled with disgust those occasional parties which his doting parents threw, whenever he had topped the merit list at school or on birthdays. How nauseating it all was; seeing those parting guests coming over and uttering their silly banal compliments! How gladly would he have liked to spit upon their faces, if he could, and go off to bed, instead of hanging around there like an idiot! They had always left him hopeless and miserable; empty, vague and lost. But, at least, they were some life-celebrating activity of sorts.

Today, he no longer had anything to look forward to. He was becoming blind to everything. Slowly, he was growing insentient beyond redemption, to many things that happened around him; especially of the careerist rat-race and the political circus that went on. He did not care to read newspapers or listen to the news. He could literally feel the outer crusts of his Being ---affection, hate, friendship and laughter, all beginning to merge into an undifferentiated mass of emotions, without a nucleus. They were all crumbling down upon him, crushing him into an unfeeling mass of self-bondage--- transforming him into a blackhole.

Now, orbit-less and abandoned, he would drift through the hazy maze of thoughts and emotions, all so diffuse and meaningless, on a motiveless voyage of Existence.

But in spite of all this abysmal gloom, there came to him, from somewhere, a strange urge, sometimes, to ask someone for help--- for advice. Even yesterday, such a demonic idea had caught him in its seductive snare. Doped by it, he had ventured to ask an elderly relative, as to what he should best possibly do. Spat came the reply. She advised him to immediately sit for the Civil Services examination, as he was already twenty-four. If he did that, he could avail of all the three chances which they gave, if need be.

(Maligaon, Guwahati, 1980)

TENDER GREEN
POMEGRANATE LEAVES

Swirling waves of passion welled up within her and held her being as she stood against the iron grill and looked out her window at the tender green pomegranate leaves, swaying freely in the morning breeze outside. It was already 8 O'clock and she was late. The staff pool bus would be there at 8:45 sharp she knew, but did not move. The whiff of the fresh morning breeze acted as an anesthetic balm upon her arid mind. A strange feeling of warm tenderness heaved at her bosom, sending a sweet sensuous feeling of languor down her spine. Her routine-addicted body suddenly became forgetful of work. It longed to get out of the grind and relax; to break free and play. As the gentle gust of wind hit her face, her mind raced back to those carefree girlhood days when everything used to be so clean, so innocent and pure. The white pleated frock flying up on the swing, the ice cream that Papa had bought her, the icing on the birthday cake; all so white ---all so clean and chaste. Yes, she had made up her mind. She wouldn't be going to the office today. Those heaps of files could very well wait. So could those slimy contractors and their fucking concocted bills! They never gave her time to breathe. She couldn't, at times, even have her Tiffin in peace. She was as much put off with their plastic smiles as the obnoxious perfumes, which their sweaty shirts exuded.

The files and the bills, the contractors and the tips, would always be there. But where on earth, would she again get this rare feeling of freshness and innocence, which she felt today? This cloudy sky…this peeping sunshine…this fresh whiff of grass; and above all, the tenderness of the green pomegranate leaves, drooping gently over with their joyful loads of red!

She quickly opened the door and came out and stepped onto the lawn. The cool dew felt sweet beneath her feet. As she walked barefoot upon the grass, with her white night-gown trailing after her, she felt, as if, an inner ablution had taken place. She suddenly felt pure and fresh once again. Clean, spotless and immaculate like a virgin Iphigenia; some unblemished Cassandra!

What if she had slept with those few men for a night or two? They meant absolutely nothing to her. Nothing more than drinking water when one was thirsty, or eating when one was hungry. She had never given herself up to anyone as yet! Nor had she surrendered her mind or body to anyone. They were still very much her own. She belonged to no one as yet. She belonged to herself alone. She was a maiden still! She was a virgin still! …. was she? … Why, of course, she was! Her mind turned wistfully to the wind for reassurance. It rustled the tender green pomegranate leaves and whispered to her that she was…she was.

An hour had crept by and she hadn't known. Hadn't realized that she had wasted such a lot of time, wandering about in the garden lawn, when there so much work left to do around the house! She had always considered household chores a big hell of drudgery, and had developed a healthy aversion towards them. How many times had her Mom to shout at her for this! A fond smile crossed her lips. Poor old Mom….What a sweet woman she was! She was so simple and gullible like all those belonging to the old school; and sometimes Purnima had felt a genuine pity for her. How she would busy herself with a hundred and one household chores; cleaning, brushing, rubbing, polishing, washing and re-washing, then going all over it again, till the last speck of the stubborn stain or dirt was removed! And after having finished all that, how she would still manage to gather up the energy to go out for marketing and shopping, and feel so elated about it all! All that energy and gusto, although admirable, in a way, had no effect on Purnima whatsoever. She somehow failed to appreciate her mother's spirited obsession with all such mundane stuff. But these were necessary things, after all. Weren't they? A woman should learn and know how to take proper care of the house. Wasn't it she, who had to take up the responsibility of rearing the children, with dedication, tenderness and love? She was the gardener… they the young plants. She giggled to herself, swaying her hands in a childish happy way, and clapping. She smiled all to herself, and gave forth a long deep sigh. She wasn't sad though… Wasn't sad that she wasn't married as yet, and had no regrets whatsoever. But then how does one cope with all those foolish desires, which the dumb heart goes on desiring, despite the repeated snubs? Especially that undying desire to be loved and understood; at least by one, from the teeming millions overcrowding the world, and driving it to a point of suffocation! But strangely, in spite of her best efforts, it had always been frustration and rebuffs all the way. By now she had quite come to live with them. She had stopped crying, a long time ago. The rare sad sobbing, that welled up within, at least, did not show up in her eyes any more. She suddenly jerked her head and giggled, and looked listlessly at the rush of pedestrians and vehicles that passed her by. She felt a deep pity for them all; as they too, she was sure, would have felt the same for her. She suddenly felt a deep craving desire creep up within her and she decided, on the spur of the moment, that she would go and meet Bhaskar today. Come what may; she had to meet him today. Why? She too had a claim over him, after all! Didn't she? So what, if he was already married now! He had been her lover too, once. Besides, he was now separated from his wife, although they had not gone in for a formal divorce as yet. Marriage was, after all, just another stupid social institution which could neither establish nor sever the bond of true minds. It was the mind which was important. The union of bodies was but a sham. It was the marriage of minds which truly mattered, in the long run. It was the Mind …the Mind. Who could ever rein in, The Mind? It has always remained free. Free to roam, free to fantasize; free to reach orgasmic peaks of fulfillment with someone else, even while the body lay ensconced within the arms of another.

She was quite certain that, at least, in some remote corner of Bhaskar's mind, she was there and would continue to remain so, even as Bhaskar remained in hers. Experiences are never lost. They formed a sort of an indelible footage which one could rewind and replay at will, whenever or whatever one wanted to. She would be doing just that, today. She wasn't going to demand anything much from him; just a day's company; that's all. He owed her that much of time, at least, didn't he? She would compel him to give her that, if need be. She smiled and giggled to herself and again looked at the crowd of people and vehicles passing her by. The devilish idea gave her a tremendous thrill, and she ran indoors to have a quick bath and get ready.

Out on the road the breeze was strong. It held her white printed sari tightly pressed against her body, making a fine cleavage between her thighs as she walked fast, down the row of trees that lined the edge of the large pond that lay beside the women's college, where she had been a student once. She could sense the force of the wind insistently brushing against her taut nipples and gliding down her thighs. The new pair of bras was making her feel a little uncomfortable. She should have, perhaps, worn them a little loose. The panties were fine though. They fitted her perfectly, and made her feel good and cozy around the pubis. She had looked splendid in that blue color in front of the dressing room mirror. She was sure that Bhaskar would have some comment to pass. Blue, she knew, was his favorite color. She just couldn't fathom why even his cursory remarks and the most casual of gestures sent a rippling wave of affection through her, conveying a feeling of deep intimacy. Was this, what they called, Love? His physical closeness aroused a wild gale of passion in her. No other man excited her as much as he. The sight of his bare chest and stunted nipples, sent a raging flame through her soul, and she would, perforce, come to feel that he belonged to her alone and that she loved him very much; loved him immensely. Strange as it might seem, even with all her clothes on, she would sometimes feel, as if, she was completely naked in front of him; her natural female resistance just melting like wax before his hot scorching embrace.

She suddenly realized that she was walking very fast, and her face was all wet with perspiration, in spite of the wind which was still blowing strong. She secretly prayed that Bhaskar would be at home today and not gone off on some official tour or something. Today was Friday, he should normally be there. She hoped he was not angry with her still. Misunderstandings do take place everywhere. Even those, so called, happily married couples go on misunderstanding each other, and quarrelling over it time and again. One should not take such things seriously! After all, why should one? Wouldn't it be downright foolish to waste precious time on such silly matters as these? She was sure Bhaskar would understand, and had forgotten about it all by now. The guy in her bedroom that day was, in fact, a distant cousin of hers. How could she have opened the door and let Bhaskar in, when he was there? Bhaskar had misunderstood her action, and was very, very angry. He had simply refused to take her calls, when she had tried to explain. Although, he must have felt very much let down then, later he must have understood her awkward predicament. That's why he had sent her that card saying "It's OK". After all this while, he would hardly remember such a petty matter or make any issue of it. He should know how much she needed him; how badly she had been missing him all this while! He must know that he was one of the rarest things that ever happened to her in life. She always had a feeling that, in spite of all his wayward lifestyle and light talk, he too liked her; liked her body, at least. Else how could he have enjoyed with her so much in bed, the way he did? He couldn't have done that with everyone! Or could he?

The long stony flight of steps, leading up to Bhaskar's bungalow on the hillock, was strewn with fallen leaves. The wind was aimlessly sweeping them around. She stood at the bottom and hesitated. Should she go up or no? He was there. His car was there. But would it be the right thing for her to do? To suddenly land upon him that way, with no prior hint whatsoever! Will he be glad to see her? Would she feel disturbed? What if he had some engagement already lined up for the day? What if there were guests? What …what … if there were some girl? Thoughts whirled within her head, as madly as the wind which rustled among the tall trees around. She just did not know what to do… what to decide. Go in or no? No! She should go in. After coming all this way, after missing the office, after giving everything else a go by for the day, wouldn't it be downright stupid and cowardly of her, to go back just like that? Besides, who knew if she would ever get this opportunity once again? This frame of mind, this burning desire, and the wind blowing this way! She decided she would go in. Go in, she would! Worse comes to worse, he would think her a fool. What more?

She didn't press the doorbell. She knocked gently. It was more intimate, she thought. "Bhaskar! Are you in, Bhaskar?" No reply. Perhaps he was bathing, dressing up or having breakfast. Her heart gave a wild leap as Bhaskar opened the door, all wet and smiling in a striped Turkish towel. "Hello! Hi Purnima! What a surprise! Come in... Come in." He quickly removed the bunch of newspapers and clothes and cleared up the sofa for her. Purnima didn't bother to sit. Her eyes followed his frisky movements around the room. "I've come to meet you Bhaskar", she said, feeling a strong impulse to hold him close. But he kept on moving. "Sit...Sit...I'm so wet. I'll come in a minute." He quickly disappeared behind the thick silken screen of curtains, looking alluringly exciting in his bare wet athletic body and towel. What was wrong with Bhaskar? He had become so very polite and formal! Earlier he would have hugged her there and then; wet as he was, in his towel. What was the matter? Her Bhaskar wasn't like that! She involuntarily sank into the cold leathered sofa with a long sigh, and stared blankly at the large framed seascape, hanging on the wall opposite, not daring to think any further.

Fully dressed in a formal suit, with polished shoes, necktie and all, Bhaskar returned and sat down beside her on the sofa. As he took her hand, she sensed a deeper unfeeling cool in his palms, against the throbbing warmth of hers, than what the morning shower could have brought about. "Are you going out somewhere today, Bhaskar?" she asked faintly." "Oh! Yah…there's a Distributors' Meet today at the Hotel Grand. It may take the whole day. I hate these lousy business meetings, especially on weekends. But these guys won't give you a space to breathe. They pay you well, but will make sure to extract every single pie they spend on you to keep the profit margin ticking. I could have thought of some excuse before, but now being the Regional Manager, you know…" His rambling words drifted far away from her, although she could discern the same old twinkle in his eyes. A heavy stone fell on her heart. The inevitable had happened; just as she had feared. But there was nothing she could do now. She had already taken the plunge by deciding to come. "Oh! You're the Regional Manager now? Wow! That's great! I hope you do not bear any grudge against me still. Do you? I was so helpless that day. The guy was my distant cousin. We were just having coffee together. I didn't want him to know about our relationship…you know how they think and talk. Besides…" she cut off abruptly, realizing that Bhaskar was busy tidying up the papers and was not interested in what she was saying. "Oh! I see…" Bhaskar said, making a pretence of listening, to relieve the awkward silence, of the ruptured communication which had befallen. "Would you like to have a cup of hot tea or coffee? Forget all what had happened Purnima. Life is a long bumpy road, and we must all learn to move ahead. Such things do happen. It's all a part of the game…Ramen! Make us two cups of coffee. Quick!" He now came over and stood before Purnima. "Look, I'm in a bit of a hurry today…" he mewed apologetically. She stood up and put her arms gently around his neck, and looked him straight in the eye. "Bhaskar, is it really necessary that you go out just now? I have come here all the way, just to meet you…to be with you for a while…Bhaskar." She kissed him on the lips. Her tender breasts were gently nudging his chest. "Bhaskar, you know I love you. I want to spend the day with you… to be just alone with you today." "I too would have loved to do that Purnima; to spend the whole day in each other's company, and that too, after such a long time! But as I said, I have this darned meeting today, and I have to bloody hell preside over it myself! They'll all be waiting for me, you see. Come, I'll take a detour and drop you at your office, on my way. We'll meet tomorrow…a hundred percent!" She didn't say a word. She just smiled vaguely and let her arms fall limply from his shoulders, and just continued to look at him from a great distance, as if. "Tomorrow, make it tomorrow," he continued, "Where shall I pick you up from? Tell me the time…Oh! Here's the coffee! Come Purnima, don't look so downcast, a hot cup of coffee will cheer you up. And also keep you awake, in that stuffy office of yours…Ha…Ha!" "Oh! Forget it, Bhaskar", she cut him short. "Come let's go!"

As they drove down the wide road fast, past the traffic lights, past the long row of trees that lined the edge of the large pond that lay beside the women's college, where she had been a student once, and the children's park round the bend, Bhaskar went on talking, of so many things. He laughed, joked and even patted her cheeks in the open car. He whistled a tune and even hummed a song. The weather was wonderful, he said. It was an ideal day to go for an outing with her somewhere today; away from the madding crowd. But he was helpless. His hands were tied. His job would go if he did it today. He loved her very much. He would definitely make it a point to meet her tomorrow. "What time…at nine in the morning? Would it be okay?" He'd pick her up from her house. They'd go somewhere far away… far from the madding crowd…stay back for the night, if need be. They could come back early the next morning...or after breakfast...or else they could... Purnima was no longer listening.

She looked straight ahead, right through the windscreen; a vacant smile lay frozen on her pursed lips. Her expressionless face betrayed no emotion. Her mind had embarked, yet once again, on a lonely journey to that mysterious realm of silent thought and contemplation, far away from the din and logic of daily Existence; where many a time she had been before, in search of that secret solace which she found there, in the face of the most frustrating of dejections.

Bhaskar had promised to meet her tomorrow. Perhaps he would. Perhaps they would, in fact, go somewhere far away, and stay overnight too. Perhaps they would laugh and talk and go around shopping, or stop over somewhere for a mug of beer or two. Perhaps they would also be in bed together, enacting scenes of affection and intimacy or be locked in sweaty embraces, cooing template messages of love in each other's ears. Perhaps they would wash and step the AC up, and go off to sleep, in a perfect ambience of Love...

But, where on earth, would she get back her Today? This passionate and restless wind blowing so strong! This cloudy morning with its ethereal warmth of affection! This peeping glow of sunshine, so suggestive of carefree mischief and foreplay! The youthful stimulating touch of the fresh green dewy grass beneath her feet! And above all, that chaste and innocent feeling of the tender green pomegranate leaves, which hung outside her window at 8 O'clock in the morning!

(Guwahati, 1981)

WINTER

The evenings were coming on earlier these days. Perhaps, it was the beginning of winter. Crushed within a corner of the city bus, Meera was grateful for the sudden gust of cold wind that escaped through to her from the open window, and touched the back of her blouse, wet with perspiration. In spite of the general mayhem that prevailed around her, she could decipher a definite chill in the wind conveying an unmistakable hint of the advent of winter. At last, the sweltering days of summer were going to be over. The sudden touch of the cold wind ran an exhilarating feel through her. She felt her body gracefully accepting the first flow of the newborn season. Her mind raced ahead, far beyond and fast, and gave her all the feelings of mid-winter in a sweeping flash. The watery eyes, the stuffy nose, the poem they taught in school, her last visit to Shimla…all came swooping down upon her in an avalanche of nostalgia. She loved winter. It was the best of all the seasons. What could ever compare with that singular experience of a sudden chill that ran down the spine, causing a gentle shiver which gradually dissolved within the cozy warmth of the benevolent pullover? The shortening of the neck, the cat-like purring of the body and the nudging cold about the ears…Oh! She just loved winter, loved it so much.

Being a Saturday, the bus was unusually crowded; office employees mostly, going back to their nearby countryside homes for the weekend. The overpowering smell of human sweat was nauseating and her nose desperately looked for a niche to poke through and take a deep breath of fresh air. The men hovering around her seemed to have no sense of decency whatsoever. They pressed so close that she had to keep devising ingenious ways of positioning her bag and arms to fend them off, preventing them from coming into direct contact with her body. She hated this weekend commuting by bus and usually took an auto-rickshaw or share taxi to get back home from the office. But it being the end of the month, she wanted to save whatever little of the salary that was left, to cover the expenses of the last few remaining days. A big chunk of her meager savings had already been spent on the treatment of her ailing mother, and last month she had defaulted on the house loan EMI. Fate had been mostly unkind to her and she wondered when this inexorable struggle would end, if ever. Being naturally tough she had taken head on every challenge that had come her way. She had fought all through, fought relentlessly. But now she was gradually growing tired of it all, and wondered if a time would come when she would be unable to take it any longer, and just have to give it all up one day. She wasn't angry with what life had doled out to her, but rather becoming tired, very tired. Seasons had come and gone, passing her by. So many springs, so many autumns, monsoons, summers and winters! But now the winter of life was gradually setting in, and there would be no spring to follow.

Stooping down with some difficulty, she tried to look out the window to find out where they had reached. The sight of the people, from their hips downwards, the children and the hawkers on the dimly lit pavement, though a common sight, was nonetheless diverting. All these, had become a part of her existence, by now.

She passively allowed the impressions, and the images they evoked, to sink down silently into her being. Like hundred other daily nuances, these too dissolved into her sub-conscious mind, transforming her, unconsciously, day by day for good or worse. She had literally surrendered herself to them. But there was one thing which she could never reconcile herself to. Her entire being, revolted at the idea of being pushed around. It was this aspect of her nature, which made her journey to and from the office, an unspeakable ordeal. She viciously reacted to every jolt and push she had to encounter in the bus or the train, for that matter. No matter how much she tried to reason, she could never make herself come to terms with it. Ten years of commuting drudgery had not been able to soften her on this score. She stubbornly refused to be broken. She was one of those priggish dimwits, who never learnt things in life. Snail-like she remained cuddled in her own shell of a make-belief world. People like her, were doomed to suffer; doomed to frustration and defeat in the ruthless rat-race of life. She knew it well, but couldn't somehow help it. Trying to be anything different, would be like denying her very existence as an individual being. It would be like revolting against her very self. She could not allow herself to be transformed into some insentient robot like most others, whose every thought and action seemed to have been programmed, which just had to be replicated and punched into some hapless set of data-cards, as if.

How often had she taken the worst of decisions and brought down ruin upon herself and those around her, because of this nature of hers. Later, repenting of the foolhardiness, when she had tried to rectify matters, it had inevitably been, too very late. Three times, they had come with that marriage proposal, and every time how bluntly she had refused them all. The last time she literally had to play up hell. Her life had become miserable by those beseeching suggestions of her near ones, in their vain attempt to make her come round. She could never forget that vulnerable tearful look in the wrinkled face of her grandmother, that night. Even years after her death, that face still continued to haunt her dreams at night, sometimes. But what could she have done? Could she have yoked herself to someone, for whom she had not an inkling of feeling whatsoever? Why, that would have been nothing, but downright naked prostitution! What else? She wasn't on the lookout for a Marlon Brando or some Onassis. She wasn't that crazy, to try and reach for the moon! All she wanted was to be married, if she ever did, to someone for whom she had a genuine feeling or urge; someone to whom she would naturally feel propelled to give herself up to. How disgusting of her relatives, not to have understood this basic stupid fact! How could she have ever disclosed this to them?

But to be unabashedly frank, there was something more to it, than this. There was some fickle delinquency; she would call it now, which lingered in her mind then. She didn't want to get herself tied up with anyone so early. She was only eighteen and wanted to have a fling at life, for sometime more. She thought that she still could afford to indulge in the foreplay of coquetry a little longer, and so didn't appreciate the terrible hurry they were in. How sweet was that feeling of uncertainty and how full of possibilities! How rich the broad span of new promise that lurked within a future so unknown! It held all the excitement of a republican voter who kept his options open till the very last moment, flirting with his or her franchise. How drab all things became, once the vote was cast! How hopeless the frustration! How irrevocable the doom! Now, how, for all the world, could she ever have imagined, that marriage would knock at her doors for only those three times? So many of her friends have been throwing away marriage proposals and gone on flirting, changing lovers as frequently as they did their sanitary napkins! And yet, today they were all happily married, and rich. How many of them were still carrying on with their petty love-games, like nobody's business! She smiled to herself. What a paradox this life held! So many girls, so many boys; so many men, so many women, and the population near to exploding, and not one single man around, for her to get married to!

By now, she had quite reconciled herself to her fate. She also realized that her desire for getting married had actually slackened off quite a great deal, by now. For ten years she had been on her own. Her mother had just been an appendage, a scarred tissue, which would fall off any day. She could, very well, go on that way, for the rest of her life. After all, what was the need for getting involved with someone else and invite unwarranted complications into one's life? She really had neither the energy left, nor the mind, to solve problems any longer. She just wanted to passively inhale, whatsoever of life, was left for her to breathe. But, at times, she felt a strong desire to be a mother. A wan smile crossed her parched lips, as she recalled her girl-hood dreams of home-making and children. She really felt a compelling urge, sometimes, of bearing a child within her womb, feel it grow day by day, and be born. A child who would grow up and call her Mom, and in whose innocent twinkling eyes, she would perceive her world condense and revolve. But there certainly was no question of Vinod giving her that child. He had no intention, whatsoever, of marring her. She knew that too well. Neither could she ever dream of calling him her husband nor he of fathering her child, for that matter. Why, he was himself a baby still! What he actually needed, and she had often told him so, was not a wife but a mother on whose lap he could cry and pour out his woes.

Fortunately the crowd had eased off a bit and Meera managed to cleverly slide into a nearby seat. The wind was hitting her directly in the face now and she could breathe freely, although people still continued to press against her shoulder. How different was the ambience in the London Metro in which she as a child had travelled with her parents from Burnt Oak station, when they used to live at Camrose Avenue in Edgeware. They would alight at Goodge Street and walk down to Tottenham Court Road where her father taught in that Language School. They went there mostly on Fridays so that dad could join them after work, to spend the weekend. After having a hurried sandwich and a sip of the hot *café latte* at one of the roadside eateries dad would leave for work while she and mom would spend the day loitering around Oxford Street window shopping or picking up trifles of jewelry and trinkets, small mementos and souvenirs from wayside vendors, or just spend time browsing the covers of books neatly inclined on the upright racks.

Sometimes they would ramble through the garment stores around Picadilly Circus admiring the elegant party dresses and the black tuxedos, wondering how smart or odd dad would look in one of those. She was often embarrassed at the way mom would go on asking all those silly questions, boring the salesgirls to death. Then they would have lunch at one of those wayside Turkish restaurants. She particularly relished the fish and chips they served with mustard sauce. Sometimes they would order for some stuffed pita bread too when very hungry. Mom enjoyed the juicy beef steak most, which was most strange for someone brought up in an orthodox vegetarian Indian family, she thought. But mom was a person with a mind of her own. She did not go by traditions, but rather established them. She had encouraged her daughter too, to think and decide for herself instead of going along with the herd. But Meera was too tame then, and lacked the frighteningly adventurous spirit of her mother. It was only after she went to college that she too began experimenting; with foods, dresses and boyfriends. She had had a whale of a time as a hosteller, with no one to breathe down her neck all the time. She was all on her own and the world was her oyster. Her parents hadn't separated till then, and dad would go on sending her the money whenever she needed it. Mom hardly bothered except for calling up now and then, telling her of the latest thing she had done; mostly about the parties and social events she had gone to, or of the poetry recitals or exhibitions she had lately attended.

But how dramatically things had changed overnight; that big quarrel and mom suddenly walking out on dad and coming back to India to live on her own! Dad had been very upset and lonely for a long time. She could not really blame him for finally giving in and going off with the other woman and living with her in Mexico now; although she wasn't quite sure how long the relationship would last. She didn't wish to go back and live with her mom's family. How so awkward it would have been! So she had decided to give up her studies mid-way and take up this job with the sales tax department, the first to come her way, and also brought mom along to live with her. She loved the transfers initially. It enabled her to visit new places and meet new people, to divert her mind and to get rid of the boredom that loneliness brings in its wake. But the early thrill had by now quite worn off, especially by this current remote posting and the dearth of commuting facility here. Boredom had again set in. In fact, it had only helped in reawakening the loneliness which had always been there; buried deep within her heart, except for the short fling which she had with Vinod.

A deep reality struck her conscience. The short tempestuous affair which they had had a year ago, had somehow made Vinod an integral part of her being. She could not clearly comprehend how the feeling had evolved. But ever since that day they had first gone to bed together, there had been a persistent secret longing in her heart, a craving rather, for him. Being separated from him, she would suffer. She still loved Vinod although he was married now. His presence worked magic in her. His very touch sent a thrill through her body, and she could then forgive him the most heinous of crimes, with all her heart. Her body literally hungered for him. She could not think of sleeping with anyone else and get that fulfillment. He was the only one who suited her palate; going with any one else would be as tasteless and dull as chewing paper. He had, somehow, become her life-giving spring; an oasis among the desolate sands of her life, which quenched the burning desires of her mind and flesh. But 'No Marriage', he had said. And, 'No Marriage', she too had concurred.

Although she had mentally reconciled herself to the fact that Vinod and she could never be a socially accepted pair any longer, she cherished the few moments they could still steal and be together at private parties at some friend's place or large social functions and get-togethers where nobody took notice. She fondly caressed the pearl necklace on her neck, a gift from Vinod on last Valentine's Day. He loved to see her wearing it, especially with that blue plunging neck-line dress. But these days friends and their parties too had grown rarer. The Gen-Next had arrived and taken everything over --- the media, the ads, the hoardings, the food joints and the gala open rock shows to boot!

There was no place for the older generation any longer. They had to move back into their slot or suffer the mortification of being pushed down there ruthlessly, and fast. Meera wondered how her mother had gone on living her life the way she did for so long. No one had pushed her down, the way they did now. Meera sadly realized that it was past the time that she too have had settled down in life. She had always dreamt of having a cozy home of her own, the living room decorated with paintings and artifacts, a lawn where the family could unwind and the children play, alongside a tiny pond with small lotus leaves lazily floating in it. She hated the busy-bee life of her mother with seminars, meetings and exhibitions. She did not aspire to be an activist like her but a simple homemaker.

She breathed a deep sigh, half knowing that her dream would always remain a dream and nothing would ever materialize. Every passing day was only making her older. The visions of youth were fleeting past her, going farther and farther away. Things which appeared to be but at an arm's length just yesterday had slipped her by and she had literally to stretch hard to touch them even, leave alone having them within her grasp. The immensity of the speed astounded her. She was only twenty nine, but the hectic rush of the upcoming youth had already pushed her quite a few rungs down the ladder, or the escalator rather, to be more appropriate. Where in this mad rush would she be able to find a new love again? Besides, she had her mother too, to look after; who, in spite of her bold talk and enthusiasm, was growing feeble by the day. The doctor had to be called in more frequently these days, and she could well guess that it was a losing battle she was fighting. Time had overtaken

Meera and she would never be able to catch up with it again. How beautiful life had been when dad and all of them had been together! But those happy memories had all gone sepia like the old photographs that lay in a dusty corner of her study table. Her heart ached with a thousand pains but she had no one to share her sorrow with, no one to pour her heart out to.

The bus was quite empty now. Most of the passengers had found their destination and got off. There was a lot of air to breathe but the same old weary breaths to take. Just to breathe and go on living! She was trapped within an inexorable rut of washing, brushing, cooking, shopping, buying medicines for mother, taking her for check up, then back to the office and the files and the grueling commuting. She felt the sweat spreading out all over her body forming a slimy paste under her clothing. Her back was wet all over, and her blouse had become so sticky, that she couldn't even lean back on her seat. She felt disgustingly horrible. The cool breeze, which had grown stronger now, was only aiding in condensing the sweat into a settling salt, all over her ebony body.

The first thing that she would have to do, on reaching home, was to have a good bath. There were few things which were so exhilarating than giving up one's naked self to the shower. An evening bath always made her feel rejuvenated and active. She thought of the new brand of shampoo which she had bought at the mall on way to the bus stand. They said it was especially suited for dry hair, like hers. She clumsily fumbled in her shopping bag to make sure it was there, but she couldn't find it. The two cakes of soap, the toothpaste and the deodorant were all there; so was the box of medicines, but the shampoo was missing. Damn It! Where was the shampoo? She had bought it, she was sure. It was very much there, in front of her eyes, lying on the counter, when she was paying the bill in a hurry. Did that talkative sales boy forget to put it in, together with the rest of the stuff? Then it must be lying there still. She clearly remembered paying for it. The cash memo was in her purse! She felt like throwing the whole bag of shopping on that salesboy's stupid face. But, thinking of all that was silly. The question was what would she do now? Going back to the shop again was out of question. It was already late and she couldn't imagine going over the grueling journey, to and fro, yet once again. Better to take it cool! The best option would be to go to the shop, first thing in the morning, on her way to the office and enquire.

They certainly couldn't deny that she had bought the shampoo and left it behind. No, they wouldn't do that! It was, after all, a matter of only a shampoo. They wouldn't tell so big a lie for such a small thing! But one can never tell… What if someone else had taken it away without their knowledge? In that case, she would have to recreate the whole scene and recount to them the entire chain of events. Why would she lie for a mere bottle of shampoo? She could show them the cash memo, if need be. She was an old customer of theirs. They couldn't be so mean to cheat a well-meaning helpless elderly woman like her. Did they all regard her that way these days? Has she really gone that old? Had she become so helpless? How do people, who do not know her, refer to her these days? No, she certainly had to get that shampoo back! Hadn't she paid for it? It didn't come free! Did it? How she had to budget her expenses these days! There was something called business ethics, after all! She would kick up hell if they tried to act funny. She would shout at them…She would raise her voice and gather people around… She would lodge a written complaint with the distributors….She would call up the Marketing Manager personally, if need be...…She would file a case in the Consumers' Court, if things went that far.…She would.…. She would…

(Guwahati 1982)

BLACK HOLE

The thrust of the drizzle changed with the wind, and Vikram had to sit sideways to avoid it hitting him directly in the face. In doing so he had come so close to Lynette that his shoulders pressed against the back of her wet bare shoulders, the shoulders of his wife. How strange it felt! The feel of the sudden touch and the raw sensation which it aroused surprised him totally. It was like touching her for the first time. What had happened? Why did he feel this way? Had they become two strangers once again? After living two full years as man and wife, why was he today finding it difficult to look her full in the face or to meet her eyes directly? Covering his face with his hand, as if sheltering his eyes from the rain, he stole a quick glance at her. Her face was impassive. Her taut lips and nostrils were struggling hard to hold back the gush of emotions, which were pressing hard to break loose, straining the thin walls of her high-boned cheeks. She bit her lower lip as she held firmly onto Ambhi their little son, cozily nestled on her lap; his wondering eyes peering over the protective veil of her blue printed sari. Ensconced within the cramped confines of the creaky old rickshaw, Vikram comprehended the true contours of his world. Amidst the vast cosmic tides of existence, where nothing merited record other than the birth and death of stars, here was his own little world, albeit so very inconsequential. Here was the spherical lab where atoms would have to coalesce, here where the nuclei would be split.

Stars, meteors, asteroids and comets with tails of cosmic dust trailing a hundred miles behind, and the spiraling nebulae; all forever combining, forever disintegrating away! Having no will of their own, they only obey. The plan was all neatly laid out. They did not have to bother to choose or to decide. The cosmic dance of Shiva! Vikram mused. He took out his handkerchief and wiped the rain from his face to ease the tension. How neat it had all looked, for him and Lynette too, when they had met for the first time at his friend Ajay's birthday party! She was a very good dancer. She was dancing with someone else, but looking at him all the while, over her partner's shoulder and smiling. When the dance had ended she had come and sat beside him and poured out a drink for him. They began by talking of trifles. He came to know that she was an artist, teaching art at a local college. She too came to know that he was a lecturer. Their professions were the same. They appeared to have the same likes and dislikes, shared the same tastes and views and the same outlook on life. They even had similar opinions about the primary colors and about Salvador Dali. It was, as if, they had been predestined to meet, drawn together by some strong primordial force. It seemed they had finally fallen into the cosmic groove. The restless search was over. They had nothing to bother about any longer but to surrender themselves to that elemental force, which would ultimately lead them to their preordained destiny. But what had happened now? Why had everything changed so very dramatically, and over so short a period? They seemed now to disagree on every other small thing! The arguments and fights were becoming more frequent and growing worse by the day. The neighbours knew them as a quarrelsome couple, and wondered why they had ever to get married in the first place, if it was to be that way! They hardly had any answer to that. Nor could they explain why they had done it all over again, yesterday. So there they sat alongside, like two dumb idiots in the wet creaky rickshaw, with nothing to communicate to each other, nothing to say.

Vikram just failed to comprehend why Lynette had to get so worked up whenever he spoke to other women, or happened to be in their company. She should understand that from among them all, it was her whom he had chosen to be his wife and life partner. She should be aware of the preeminent place he had given her in his life and appreciate that! She should realize that she was the master cassette, the others mere replications. She was the original copy, they the duplicates. She was the mother chord; the 'Sa', they the other relative ones. While others floated in and out, she was the basic scale which held his life in tune. He half smiled thinking of the, off the cuff, remark of his friend Jai who said that wives were meant for serious business and not for such frivolous things as sex. People, who flirted with their wives, did not take them seriously, he believed. Vikram thought Jai was indeed correct. But then why did he feel so exasperated when other man spoke lingeringly to Lynette and always tended to interpret it as some form of oblique flirtation?

Feeling uncomfortable, Ambhi wriggled in his mother's lap, kicking Vikram on his knees with his tiny feet. The father and son exchanged glances and smiled. Vikram bent down and kissed the baby on the forehead. He was undoubtedly his bundle of joy. The spiky hair on his large forehead still jutted out as they had done the day he was born. The golden colour had turned a shade brownish now. It was a miracle that he had survived that day!

That day too, they had had a big fight. But later they had patched up and gone for a late night show at the local theatre, to ease the residual tension off. On coming home late and tired he had dozed off immediately on going to bed. It was around 1 O'clock at night when Lynette had nudged him awake. She had been bearing the pain for quite some time, unwilling to disturb him, at first. But now she could take it no longer. The spasms were coming on more excruciatingly. He had quickly jumped out of bed and ran downstairs to call the office driver to take out the van. As they were hurrying down the stairs Lynette had tripped on her gown and fallen out of his grip, rolling three steps down before he could pick her up again. Her arms had fallen limp and she was sweating all over. For a while she was in a complete state of shock. Instinctively he felt for her belly. There was absolutely no semblance of any movement whatsoever. "Is it moving?" she had murmured. "Yes", he lied to her. Holding her fast he helped her into the vehicle, and they had raced away towards the hospital, his mind all the while struggling to fend off the idea of the inevitable, which kept coming a hundred times over. He could hardly talk to her in the Casualty as they had snatched her from him, put her on a stretcher and taken her away. They had asked him to please stay outside. There was absolutely no place to sit as people were sleeping on all the chairs and benches in the lobby; attendants of serious patients, perhaps. So he went outside the collapsible gate, into the foggy night and was pacing to and fro, restless and apprehensive, smoking and trying to push the thought of the impending news of the inevitable away.

"Mr Choudhury, anybody...? Mr Vikram Choudhury...?" The voice of the nurse was very faint, but he had heard it clearly. His mind braced to hear the inevitable...a stillborn child…or worse. He didn't dare to move. But he must. "Yes! What's the matter? Is everything OK?" He came forward to the grilled door. The nurse looked at him amused, surprised perhaps, by his nervous tension. "She's feeling cold. Do you have some warm clothes?" Warm clothes! Where could he get any warm clothes at this hour of the night? Don't they keep any blankets in the hospital! But realizing that it was not the time to debate when the life of his wife and child were at stake; not the time to argue but to just swallow the shit, he quickly took off his pullover and handed it over to the nurse through the grill. "How's she? And the child…?" The nurse had no time for such humdrum queries. Taking the pullover she disappeared among the crowd as suddenly as she had appeared.

The next two hours out in the bitter cold were traumatic. Was something wrong? Was there an emergency? Would his child survive? Would Lynette…? Not being allowed to be with his wife when she needed him most, not being able to do anything to ensure the safety of his wife and child when anything could happen! It was all so very frustrating. He despaired to think about it and just cut out the natural chain of thought coming to his mind and diverted the track.

What a wonderful hour it was! What an experience would it be to become a father! What a sweet way to pay his debt back to Nature! How wonderful was Love! How it had brought Lynette and him, two total strangers, so close together. How it had combined their minds and bodies to continue the eternal legacy. How fulfilled they would feel! How smooth and neat. How flawless the Application programme! They did not have to think and decide. And so, there wasn't any scope of making a blunder. They just had to surrender to the programme and obey. Obey as the buds to bloom, like the fruit to ripen and fall, like the seed to germinate, obey like the stars to be born and decay. As sure and certain like lightning choosing the path of least resistance or the river blindly meandering its way unmistakably towards the sea.

Last night's quarrel had been the worst of all. They would not have been talking to each other for days had it not been for Ambhi whose booster doses were due and they had to take him to the clinic today. He had been so wild with her that he had torn to bits the beautifully framed photo which they had taken together during their honeymoon to Darjeeling, soon after their marriage, which they had to do in the court. There was no other way. The humid smell of sweat and the musty files in the cramped court room, where he had stood with Lynette, mixed with the fumes emanating from the open chlorinated urinal still hung upon his nostrils. He was sorry that he had to do that to Lynette. But he was also proud of her; the way she had stoically put up with the ordeal, her face flushed at the unaccustomed sordid atmosphere, the embarrassment and the delay.

His widowed mother and sisters were so adamant that he had no other option. How they had all started howling at him, all at a time, that other day, trying to knock some sense into his maverick brain! They couldn't imagine how pig-headed he might be to marry a divorcee, and that too from a different religion. Fed up with their unreasonable behavior and narrow-mindedness he had walked out of the house right there and then, out into the open night. It was well past midnight when he landed up at the railway station to sit the rest of the night through.

Lynette was genuinely surprised to find him knocking at her door at five in the morning. He had made her write a leave application to her college hurriedly, and by 9 O'clock they had already boarded the bus, well on their way to meet her parents and talk about marriage. Her soft-spoken father was down forthright. "You are a teacher of literature", he said, "You have studied the lives of so many people down the history, what more have I to tell you. You very well know my daughter's state in life and all what she has passed through. If you still think and decide that both of you can be happy by getting married, I can have no objection to that. But please think it over carefully. The bottom line is that you should be happy, and she too."

They weren't themselves then. Nor did they have any control over their young unfettered minds. Driven on by an overwhelmingly powerful Life-force, they had spontaneously decided then, that they would be happy. In fact, they could not have decided otherwise. They were bound by the set command of a universal program; the same that causes the yellow pollen of the anther to stick to the hairy feet of the bee and spread easefully onto the stamen.

In spite of the rain, the clinic was unexpectedly crowded. There were eleven names already listed ahead of them. He was very hungry and thought Lynette too must be feeling the same, both having skipped dinner last night. Ambhi had already had his morning quota of cereals and it would not be wise to feed him anything now. He thought of venturing the question to her, but refrained. Usually it was she who was the one who proposed about eating whenever they went out. Lynette loved to eat out while he preferred home made dishes.

Lynette was a good cook but a little less than his mother, he thought. But over the last two years he had grown quite used to her cooking and secretly craved for them, especially the Chinese stuff. She really did them well. Lynette, however, loved the *dhaba* food and all that *roti* and spicy *tarka* which they served, rustically embellished with chopped onions, long green *chillies* and *achar*. It was in one of these roadside joints that they had come across Rohan, a former college mate of hers. He was uncomfortably loud and Vikram cringed at every move of his. He was downright outraged when Rohan while leaving had suddenly bent over and gave her a parting peck on her cheeks. The handle had flown off the bar! He had picked up a glass full of water and splashed it full on her face before everyone and drove off in a huff, leaving her stranded on the highway. But the field of attraction was still going strong then. They had afterwards talked it over, patched up and held each other close, in reaffirmation of the inextricable bond that existed between them, and made love.

But what had happened now? They were neither moving forward or back! He could neither leave nor continue staying with her. It was so very strange! Although it seemed sometimes that they had had enough of each other, yet somehow it felt that they still belonged to each other and were destined to be together forever. One just could not break free of the other, being held together by a forceful inseparable bond, except through mutual destruction, as if. He knew that it would be impossible to imagine a life without her, and she too must be feeling that way. Else why, a strong-minded independent woman like her, was not walking out on him, as she had done the first time? He too could very well have divorced her. In, fact, all his relatives and well wishers would have welcomed the move. But then, what about Ambhi? How could they both do that to him? They had given him birth. He had evolved out of their union. He was the new star that was born. For him, if not for anything else, they would have to revolve around him together, go on revolving and gradually fade; continuing to give whatever light and warmth that was left within their own Chandrasekhar limit, until such time when consciousness ceased to take cognizance of the self any longer and transformed itself to oblivion, to lurk somewhere in the deep elongated recesses of some dark monstrous black hole.

(Guwahati 1984)

THE IMMERSION

The sound of the drums came wafting across the window, sometimes staccato and sometimes a rolling rumble, reaching a crescendo and then carried away again by the rain-soaked late September wind, to the suburban lanes below. Reclining on her hospital bed, Reena could clearly sniff the fragrance of incense pervading the festive air outside, along with the rancid stench of chlorine and urine, emanating from the open WC doors of the general maternity ward of the Civil Hospital. It was *Dashami*, the last day of the five-day long celebration of Durga Puja, when they would be taking the Mother Goddess along with the entourage of her four divine children (with whom she visits her earthly home annually), in a grand procession for their final immersion in the river; along with her lion-mount, the demon Mahisasur whom she had slaughtered, et al.

In spite of herself, Reena's heart was beating furiously away; keeping a strange rhythm with the drum beats outside, and her mind was swaying wildly to the erratic movement of the wind, which splashed drizzles upon the broken window pane near her bed. Suddenly she seemed to have been caught in the vortex of some momentous cosmic movement that brings about Life and Death in the Universe...the forces of Creation, Preservation and Destruction. The imposing image of the ten-armed Goddess Durga zoomed in and out of her mind in rapid succession, engulfing her totally in its splendorous majesty and dazzling array of glittering arms. She lay motionless, as if in a stupor, for some time. But as consciousness crept slowly back, she once again became aware of the faint rattling sound of the drums in the distance. And then, of the wind…the chlorine stench mixed with the fragrance of incense…and the nagging sound of the rain.

They had bought her there in a terrible state last night. The placenta had ruptured, and her clothes were all wet from the profuse bleeding. She hardly remembered what followed next, except for the doctor in the green mask, the nurses rushing about with the disposable syringes, the canola being pushed into her nerve, and the saline bottle hanging above her head. And, of course, the pain…the excruciating pain which came on in spasms at increasingly frequent intervals; till the final cataclysmic agony, when she finally delivered the child.

But now, looking back, it had all been such a wonderful experience! The sheer happiness that arose in her heart, watching her bundle of joy, huddled cozily beside her, more than doubly compensated for the trauma she had to go through. Her illiterate mother had been very right when she had told her never to trust a man fully. But, how for all the world, could she have imagined that Vinod would ditch her this way? They had been meeting each other for over three years now, and their love had seemed to be growing stronger by the day. She had been looking forward to a new life, which she had never known, but only dreamt of. And it seemed, that her dream was nearing fulfillment. They would be having a small loving family of their own, content with whatever little they had. She would finally bid goodbye to that dingy hole, which had been her home for the last eighteen years, where she had seen nothing but drunkenness, quarrels, angst and sorrow.

Her father never loved her mother and would spend, most of the evenings, away from home. He would come back very late, fully drunk and unable to walk steadily, and slump into bed without dinner, oblivious of the curses her mother threw at him, and rise the next morning, have a cup of black tea, which Reena made for him and leave for work at the railway station, before the rest of the family had woken up. Then followed the usual round of washing and cooking, bathing the younger siblings, feeding them and sending them off to school; barefooted and in dirty uniforms, with slates and books clutched close to their chests. Their pair of uniforms, being only one, had to rough it out the whole week, and could be washed only on Saturday evenings.

Five children and the parents, seven in all, had to run the whole month on a single gang man's salary, which itself was much emaciated with pay cuts for unauthorized absence. The bulk, of whatever was left, went into paying off the credits, accrued at the ration shop and the country liquor den. Reena herself possessed little else besides the two pairs of school uniform saris, which they had bought her when she was in class seven, and the silk sari which she had received as a gift, when they had performed the religious ritual on her attaining puberty. Of course, there was also that cherished small transistor set that Raghu *mama* had given her, on which she avidly listened to the latest Hindi film songs and shampoo advertisements. This was the only purple patch of romance in her life; the only outlet to her otherwise overwhelmingly frustrating youth.

Raghu *mama*, in fact, was their only link to the world outside. He used to visit them, mostly in the afternoons, when only she and her mother would be in the house. From him they would come to know of what all was going on in the world outside. He was some ten years younger to her father, perhaps her mother's age; but looked much younger, in spite of his full bearded face, which gave him the uncanny look of some smalltime Marxist politician or a struggling artist.

He always carried a red sling bag on his shoulders and was impeccably dressed in neat white *kurta-pyjamas*. He relished mother's cooking and was always full of the profoundest praise for her culinary art. Her mother had adopted him as her brother by tying the sacred *rakhi* on his wrists; and by virtue of that license, he would often enter the kitchen and hug her playfully from behind, and they would all laugh and giggle as her mother chased him around with a spatula or a ladle. And then, they would have black tea with the sweets and the salty *namkeens*, which he would invariably bring, whenever he visited them. Reena secretly admired Raghu *mama*, and considered him to be the quintessential Man. He was always full of verve and energy; so much unlike her father. His arrival brightened up the very atmosphere of the house. Even their ramshackle hovel of a house was transformed into a home, for the while, when he was around. Of late, he had begun taking extra interest in her, she had noticed. Perhaps, it was because she was growing up, and was beginning to understand what all he spoke of, of the outside world. He would tell her of his experiences at Delhi, Calcutta or Mumbai, where he went for meetings and rallies; of how fast life was in the metropolises, and how women moved about openly and mixed freely with men at parties, and had so much fun. He had also volunteered to help her with her studies, as she was preparing for the final high school examination, and the family couldn't afford to engage private tutors for her at home.

He was brilliant, especially in math and science; subjects which most students abhor, and which she herself found so insurmountably daunting. Unlike the teachers at school, he was very patient with her, and would laugh instead of getting wild, at the silly mistakes she made. Sometimes, when she would get frustrated and burst into tears, unable to grasp some algebraic formula for the umpteenth time, he would get up from his seat and sit beside her and hold her very close to him, and reassure her that all would be fine; she shouldn't unnecessarily get so worked up, and would understand everything gradually. She really loved those soothing moments. No one in her family, not even her parents, had given her that feeling of care and concern for a very long time. How confident she would feel in his strong reassuring embrace! He would lovingly wipe away her tears, smooth her hair, and hold her tender cheeks close to his bearded ones, as a baby. Being the eldest of five siblings, she had missed much of that in her later childhood and had secretly craved for. He too, must have read her mind; for the embraces had become more frequent. In fact, sometimes when her mother would go away to buy vegetables from the nearby market, after serving them black tea, he would get up from his chair and come over and sit beside her on the bed and teach her from there. He would take her hand in his and squeeze them gently, as he went on showing the cross-section of the shoe flower, and explaining its reproductive parts. She would involuntarily find herself yielding to his warm embrace, his large palms casually straying onto her young budding breasts, sending a sudden pulse of lightning to her head. Her shoulders would go limp on the impact, and her hand would involuntarily loiter around his muscular thighs and come to rest tentatively on his throbbing groin. The sound of her mother's approach would break the blissful trance, and they would both hurry back to their respective accepted positions, of teacher and pupil.

Lying on one side for so long on the raised hospital bed, her left arm had gone totally numb. She slowly turned and lay on her back now, to ease the discomfort. Feebly grabbing the pillow, she made a desperate attempt to pull its edge onto the window sill next to her bed, to have a better view of what all was going on outside. A whiff of fresh incense-laden breeze greeted her nose. A small crowd was gathered around the *puja pandal* below. She could see children, dressed in their crumpled puja best, holding gas balloons and toy pistols, running all around.

She fondly recalled her childhood days. Her father had been quite different then. He used to be slim and smart. On puja days he would invariably dress in clean white *kurta-pyjamas* and take her around from *pandal* to *pandal*, and buy the best balloons and toys for her, giving all his love, care and time to her, being the only child then, her siblings had not been born as yet. How confident and happy she had felt! That joy would never return to her again she knew. How soon everything changes! And how so very suddenly! Perhaps, this was the essence of Life. All just touch and go. Situations change, people grow older, perspectives change, relationships change...feelings change. And soon the strong vibrant colors of life dissipate into undistinguishable strains of grey. Life drifts on and on, with no interesting thing happening for weary stretches on end.

Vinod had come like a whiff of fresh air into her life; nay more like a strong gale, which had swept her off her feet. What a whirlwind of an affair they had had! The speeding bike rides, the precarious climb up the waterfall, the night spent together at the wayside resort during the last pujas, when she had lied to mother that she was staying overnight at a friend's place!

Although he did not appear as steady and grounded as Raghu *mama*, Vinod did have that strong masculine attraction that could floor any young girl. He was an embodiment of all verve and energy. And above all, he was young. Someone more akin to her likes and dislikes; someone whom she could naturally relate to. (Raghu *mama* spoke a little too over her head). How they seemed to share so much in common! In fact, it appeared, they had been made for each other. They were destined to meet and to be together, in this life and for all lives to come, throughout the cycle of rebirths, for generations on end.

She wistfully fiddled with the ring that he had slipped into her ring finger, as an expression of love and promise…. But what had gone wrong all on a sudden? Why hadn't he turned up even after long three months? Was he in some problem? Why had he ditched her like that, knowing full well that she was already carrying his baby? He said everything was ready and there was nothing to get so worried about. That they would be getting married that day; that he had already taken a house on rent. Why then had he failed to turn up at the temple, where he had asked her to elope and wait for him? What had gone wrong? Why had he done so? Where was he now? Were the rumours, that he had eloped with another girl and was now in Nepal, true, after all? They had had a fight that day alright. But that was because he was so very drunk, and she hated drunkenness. She did not want a repeat of the trauma she had undergone all these years. She did not want to be yet another woman, yoked to a drunkard husband, like her mother. She always had a creepy foreboding feeling that drunkenness was, in someway, associated with the loss of affection. She wanted to nip it in the bud. She had a dream for her future family. A dream quite different from the life she had experienced.

A life of Love and Affection…of Unity and bonding among all the members of the family! A bond between the wife and the husband, a bond between the children and their parents…a bond of Love…a bond of Joy! But there was no reason for Vinod's mother to tell a lie! Why would she? She had come all the way looking for him to their house the other day! Wasn't it she who had mentioned about the other girl and Nepal?

It was Raghu *mama* and the neighbours who had brought her to the hospital last night. Her mother just couldn't bear the shame. But how could Vinod have been so cruel? Not even bothering about his own wife and child! Do men get tired of their wives that fast? Were all men like that? Was her mother's case, not just an exception, but the rule? Tears involuntarily rolled down her wan cheeks, and she slowly wiped them with the edge of the white bed sheet, held clumsily in her needled hand. Although she struggled with her thoughts and tried to suppress the facts, trying hard to disbelieve, deep within her, the Truth was steadily emerging and pressing against her wounded heart, rubbing the inevitable in. The naked truth was that Vinod had left her. He had found a new love and had eloped with her to Nepal. He would never come back… And, what if he ever did? The seed of mistrust had already been sown! He had already committed a serious breach of Trust, and broken the sacred bond of marriage. The fissure had appeared. The solid rock, on which all relationships stood, had been split asunder! It would never rejoin again. Not in this life; not in the cycle of rebirths of generations to come!

They were giving her a swab when mother appeared at the door in the late morning. She looked sleepless and disheveled, having to hurry through the household chores, to come there. Raghu *mama* was with her. Clasping her hand in a tight grip which spoke everything, she lisped "Everything will be OK, my child, don't worry, just rest". The mother's eyes met the daughter's. There was a deep silence; a silence which spoke more than words. Spoke of trust and betrayal, of hope and frustration, of the tremendous mortification, pain and suffering which every woman bore, down the generations; throughout the relentless cycle of births and deaths. Raghu *mama* stood silently beside her. He didn't speak a word. Perhaps he had nothing to say. She had committed a big blunder, for which there could be no redemption, but only consequences to suffer. He held her hand in a firm reassuring grip, as if to give her the courage, which she would badly need, to go through the bleak future that was in store for her. They both looked at each other; and, for a moment, an outrageous idea flashed through her mind. May be, Raghu *mama* could agree to marry her, after all, and give an identity to her child! But the thought died down instantly in an embarrassing blush, as he suddenly let go his grip. Her hand fell limply back onto the hospital bed, and she realized her hopeless situation, like some drowning person looking for a straw, to cling on to. She was hoping against hope, when, in fact, there was nothing left to look forward to.

A deep sense of remorse welled up within her breast, as she thought of poor old dad. She did not want to burden him further. And think of the embarrassment! How would she be able to live in that house ever again? She had now to fend for herself and the child, all alone. There was no one in this world, to whom, she could turn to. And why should anyone help her, in the first place? It was she who had committed the blunder, and so must suffer the consequences herself! What right had she to bother anyone else, or to meddle with their lives? No, she would do nothing of that sort! Mother had brought along, some fruit and a bag of clothes. But it was a routine exercise, which carried no feeling with it. Like they carry bouquets or fruits to some bereaved family. Just a routine social exercise; nothing else!

It was almost 5:30 in the evening when she woke up from the half conscious stupor. She vaguely recalled what all mother and Raghu *mama* had spoken, when they were there. She had been in a sort of trance, all the while, not even fully able to respond when mother had kissed her goodbye and gone. She would come tomorrow, she had said. It was already late and she would have to catch the last bus home, as the children were there alone, and she had to cook dinner for them and father. Raghu *mama* too, had bid her goodbye, wishing her well. Now she was all alone; she and her baby.

Instinctively she turned on her side. Cuddled beside her, wrapped in faded hospital linen, lay her baby all asleep; like an innocent flower that had naively bloomed amidst a hedge of thorny bushes. It wasn't aware of anything, alright. But she was. So how could she remain a silent spectator to its misfortune? Or act as if, nothing untoward had happened! She gave him a long lingering look; picked him up in her arms and began showering kisses on him, till she thought she would go mad. Suddenly she let go of him and laid him back on the bed beside her. Vaguely staring at the ceiling, she went on thinking…thinking and wondering. She smiled to herself. So, she was a mother now! The motherhood that all women dream of, some time in their life! She couldn't believe that she had become a mother so soon. This child would be her world now… she vaguely mused…she his Universe. But what a Universe!

Desperately she tried to arrive at some decision. But she just couldn't. So many terrible thoughts came to her mind that she dared not to think of them. Here was her child, her first born boy child, as innocent as a flower! How could she ever think of doing any harm to him? Let the world do or say whatever it liked, she would not part with him, at any cost. The thought of leaving him in some *ashram* or orphanage came to her. But she immediately cursed herself, a thousand times, for being so heartless to be able to think so. No! She wept, and kissed the child once more. She certainly would not do anything so cowardly against an innocent child! But then, how could she ensure a life of dignity for him? She hardly cared about herself or what would happen to her. But how could she, being a mother, deliberately abandon him to an abysmal world, wherefrom he would be cursing her one day! How could she put him up for the jeering gaze of people? To be the laughing stock of fools! No! She had no right to do that. An uncomfortable sense of guilt began to form in her mind. If this child ever suffered, it was she who would be solely responsible for it. It would be she who would be answerable for every tear he shed...for every pang he felt within his tender heart! She held the child close to her breast in a crushing embrace, and then let him go free again.

The drizzle outside had now stopped. The drums were beating louder than ever. She could hear the jubilant screams and shouts of the people, as they were taking down the deities from their pedestals and loading them onto the trucks, which would carry them to the river *ghat*, for the sacred Immersion ceremony. How fast the years had rolled by! It seemed to her, as if, it was just the other day, when she was one among the people; an integral part of the social milieu. But now, how suddenly everything had changed! It was unbelievable! Till yesterday, she shared the same common pulsating vibes that ran through the community. And today, here she was; a completely desolate soul! An abysmal gulf had arisen between her and society, and she was at a loss to find a way to overpass the same. Clasping the forefinger of her grandpa once, lost among the crowd of worshippers, how her tiny heart had admired the remarkable courage of Goddess Durga. What a singular inspiration for womanhood She was! What a manifest assertion of *Shakti*! The latent power of womanhood, grandpa had explained, was tremendous. Once aroused, it could annihilate the toughest of opponents. It was, in fact, the Female force, which fosters all Life in the world ----- The Prime Force which both creates and nurtures the world! That was why She was worshipped by all. That was why even a powerful and menacing demon, like Mahisasur, could not withstand her most formidable power!

A crooked smile crossed Reena's lips, as she leaned forward upon the wet window sill, and gazed down upon the noisy processions, and the chain of decorated trucks coming from different localities, passing along the main road, on their way to the river-bank *ghat*. She took a deep breath. She still felt weak, but that nauseating feeling had thankfully gone. As the illuminated statues passed by, Reena wondered what sort of demon, had Mother Durga actually killed. What Evil had She annihilated? What were the people so jubilant about? What sort of Deliverance had She brought? She abruptly checked herself from pondering over such blasphemous thoughts, and quickly shut her eyes devoutly in prayer. "Mother Durga", she prayed, "forgive my sinful thoughts, and give me your strength". Her hair rose on end, as she suddenly felt inspired by a bizarre thought. It did not take a concrete shape immediately, nor could she fully realize its implications, right then. But she could clearly perceive that it was gradually taking some definite shape in her mind. And before she could realize, it had possessed her completely and had her in its throes. The idea was congealing rapidly, like some vast wayward nebula, homing in upon a new-found nucleus. She could actually feel it building up in her head, as she had felt the child growing in her womb. Reena found herself no longer drifting in an ocean of chaos and confusion, but, ever so slowly, proceeding towards a definite goal. Once again, she was inexorably drawn into the powerful vortex of those Forces, which determine the event horizons of the Universe.

Thick incense smoke was now flowing freely into the room, driven by the strong evening breeze which was blowing in from the river. The rumbling of the drums was growing louder and louder along with the rising chant of the *mantras*, coming from the blaring mikes below. She called for the nurse and asked her to take the saline tubes off, so that she could go to the washroom.

She felt very weak. But nevertheless, she slowly sat up and slid off the bed, and sauntered towards the window ledge. The crowd on the street below had now swelled to a restive mob, engrossed in festive dance and revelry. The long row of decorated trucks, were creeping by, carrying the huge earthen idols of the deities and the monstrous demon king, *Mahisasur*. Even from that distance, Reena could clearly see the Mother Goddess, mounted on one of the trucks, looking gorgeous in her scintillating red attire. Resplendent with the array of shimmering arms, held in each of her ten mighty hands! Her sharp piercing eyes, exuding a sense of awesome power and purpose! She had come into this world to destroy Evil, when it had crossed all bounds of sanity. In this warlike form, she was indeed the embodiment of *Shakti*---the latent power, strength and courage, which resides in every woman...in every mother! Reena's mind began to move fast. She was weak, no longer! The power of the Goddess Durga had taken hold of her. Feeble and desolate, as she was, a moment ago, Reena now was all full of determination and purpose.

The general mood of gaiety and merriment, which was prevailing outside, seemed to have also infected the painful wards of the Civil Hospital. All the patients, who could move somewhat, were making a beeline for the terrace or the open windows, to have a glimpse and *darshan* of the Mother Goddess. Taking advantage of the confusion, Reena quickly rummaged through the bag of clothes, which mother had brought her in the morning, and fished out the red sari, which she had worn the day of her aborted marriage with Vinod at the temple, and rushed to the washroom to change.

She wasn't crying any longer. Her chiseled features froze into a singular mould of determination, and a sense of purpose sparkled from her erstwhile forlorn eyes. Rushing out of the washroom, she picked up the baby in a sharp swift movement and stood upright, motionless, for a moment, holding him in her arms in the dim-lit hospital room; looking resplendent in her red gilded sari....Defiant as Mother Durga herself!

Walking, as if in a trance, she deftly climbed down the stairs; and before she had known, was out in the streets, jostling with the reveling crowd and merging in its restless flow. She didn't have to consciously walk, any more. The crowd was, of itself, pushing her along. Holding the baby close to her breast, her feet involuntarily marched in tune to the rhythmic beat of the drums, her head held high; high as anyone else's. She moved ahead, like a woman possessed; driven forward by a terrific force of Destiny.

When the procession had reached the bank of the river, the bulk of the crowd slowed down and stepped back at a safe distance; but Reena walked on ahead with the volunteers, to the very edge of the river, from where they would be throwing the idols, over the brink. "Ma Durga… Ma Durga!" she lisped continuously, holding the child close to her bosom.

As they were throwing the lesser deities, one after the other, into the water, shouts of "Durga Mai Ki Jai!" rent the air. The faltering drums which had fallen silent, had once again, found their rhythm, and now struck up a lively beat. Reena silently stepped into the water, raising her folded hands to her forehead in adulation. A volunteer tried to push her back, asking her not to come so close. But Reena was unaware and no longer listening. Her entranced eyes lay fixed upon the eyes of the Mother Goddess, caught up in a powerful magnetic field, as if.

The drummers were working up a frenzied finale beat now. The whole atmosphere was surcharged with the emotion of religious fervour. Chants of mantras mingling with the flowers and the smoke of incense, created an aura of sanctity around the *ghat*. Devotees were thronging, in large numbers, and dropping offerings into the water, seeking the parting blessings of Ma Durga. Reena had no incense or flowers to offer. She rushed forward into the swirling waters, holding her new-born babe aloft, as an offering. The river was holy, they say. Even Mother Durga immerses herself in it, year after year, carrying away all the woes of the world, having delivered it from the forces of Evil.

As they left the last hold on the mighty statue of the Goddess, it fell into the river with a huge splash, forming rings of water all around. Reena walked with sticky feet right into the pool, neck-deep in the water now, holding the baby close to her bosom. "Goddess Durga!", she murmured, "Do not leave me alone and depart. I am utterly soaked in Evil. There is a shadow of Evil in my child too! It is a product of Evil. Mighty Destroyer of Evil! Don't leave this speck behind. Take us with you too! Oh Mother! I want to expiate for my Sin...."

The Immersion was over. The volunteers were scurrying back from the waterside; and in the general din no one had noticed anything untoward. As the rattling drums were beating the final retreat, Reena's inert body and that of her child, were both gently flowing down the river, onward to a new world, leaving the curse of Evil behind forever, hopefully to be reborn, pure and innocent once again, sometime in the future, in the ever flowing tide of times.

(Guwahati 1991)

SITUATION UNDER CONTROL

The Chief Minister was visiting our Sub-Division. Naturally, the entire Law & Order machinery had to be geared up. The Deputy Commissioner had asked the magistrates and all other departmental officers to report at 1:00 pm sharp at the Inspection Bungalow of the Public Works Department at a place called Donkamukam, some thirty-five kilometers downhill from the Sub-Divisional headquarters at Hamren, for the final review and briefing.

The Sub-Divisional Officer, who had been already on the move since morning with sundry errands and being otherwise engaged, had asked the two of us (Executive Magistrates) to attend the meeting. So we were ready and all agog and waiting. Waiting and waiting and waiting…out waiting Ol' Becket himself, while nothing ever seemed to happen. The two requisitioned vehicles just failed to show up. But still we were undeterred and continued our resolute wait. At long last at around 12:30 in the afternoon an old decrepit haggard of a jeep belonging to the Agriculture Department arrived. The driver, who looked even older, informed us that the O.C. (Officer-in-Charge of the local police station), was still on the lookout for the other vehicle. Since we were already very late and just had half an hour left to reach the meeting venu, we decided to take off immediately, both of us together, in the same 'available' vehicle, leaving instructions for the other vehicle to follow, if it ever turned up, that is.

The meeting at the Inspection Bungalow was very brisk and businesslike. The young and energetic Deputy Commissioner assigned duties and outlined the various possibilities of sabotage by insurgents, and the precautions we were to take and measures we were to adopt, in case of eventualities. We were directed to invariably send hourly SITREPs (Law & Order Situation Reports) from the nearest police stations and our walkie-talkie sets, to apprise the Deputy Commissioner of the actual situation on the ground. Thus amply briefed, we turned homeward to get ready and suitably equip ourselves for the ensuing Law & Order duty for the entire night. Since our responsibility lay in securing the long stretch of the lonely hilly terrain which the VVIP was to take, we had absolutely no time to waste. So we decided to take the shorter deserted route that cut directly across the hills back to the HQ at Hamren, instead of the normal circuitous one through which we had come in the afternoon, thus reducing the travelling distance by 12 kilometers.

The decision though seemingly a smart one was fraught with rueful consequences. After speeding deftly along for a kilometer or so there was a loud explosion which shattered the pristine silence of the verdant hills around, sending the wayside wild fowls scurrying for cover, and we began skidding sideways. The tube of the rear wheel had burst. Not to be overawed, we quickly jumped out and got the wheel replaced by the spare one. We wasted some precious 20 minutes in the process. But that did not seem to be too big a problem, as we could easily make it up by going at double the speed. After cruising along smoothly for some 3 Kilometers or so, yet another explosion! The spare wheel too had burst. We had still some 15 kilometers to go and we were totally at a loss for ideas as not a vehicle seemed to pass that way wherefrom we could get some help. Being at our wits end, thus marooned, we finally decided to roll ahead on the punctured wheel itself, come what may! And so we wobbled and hobbled, slowly yet hopefully…

After bumping clumsily along thus for another 2 kilometers or so, the flattened tyre could take it no longer; and the driver had perforce to bring the vehicle to a grinding halt hitting the side of the hill in the process, entwining us in a surrealistic mesh of broken branches, thorny creepers and wild thicket. Having somehow extricated ourselves from the mess, we checked and found, to our utter dismay, that half the wheel tube was encircling the tyre, when it should have been the other way round. So we just stood there and thought…thought and thought; thinking against Thought itself. Still some 12 kilometers left to go, and it was already getting dark! We still had to hunt for the other vehicle which had failed to turn up in the afternoon, have our grub, collect our warm clothes and other essentials and then set off for the night-long Law & Order duty ahead… thirty-five kilometers downhill yet again.

We just stood on the road aghast. Here we were; Magistrates entrusted with responsible Law & Order duty to ensure the safety of the VVIP during his rare trip to our remote Sub-Division, standing helpless as two children lost in the woods; our magisterial powers hovering above our heads like the idle wind swerving wildly among the bamboo bushes. The lonely stretch where we were stranded was known to be frequented by tigers and all sorts of wildcats. As darkness grew, our very own security was becoming a matter of concern, leave alone that of any VIP or VVIP.

In utter exasperation, we now decided to replace the dismembered wheel with the earlier punctured one and trundle along as we had done before on punctured tyres.

Inflated tyres having become a mirage, we discovered new hope in supine punctured ones. But it just didn't happen to be our day. Once again, the hapless tyre, which we had so hopefully fitted, gave way. It failed to hold the tube inside for long, and soon it curled up around the tyre in a frightening mass of warm tangled rubber. There was nothing left to do. We now had two clear choices before us; either to grope the remaining distance blindly through the forest or to ride on the bare rim. The fiery sparks which the Deputy Commissioner's meeting had ignited in our minds were fast turning to ambers. Thirst and desperation had driven the color from our lips. As the driver hopelessly fiddled with the dead tyres, we sat on a wayside stone sunk in deep thought, more akin to coma.

We must have remained that way for some half an hour or so, when our elongated ears, honed by desperate expectation, picked up the welcome whirr of a motor. And soon enough, we spied a gypsy van do the sharp bend below and zoom up towards us in a grateful benedictory flood of dazzling headlights.

As the vehicle stopped, we came on to the road and found that it was our patronizing good old friend the SPDO (Sub-Divisional Police Officer), on his way to VVIP duty downhill. He too had his hands all full with assignments and was hard pressed for time. But our pathetic state must have touched a soft cord in his boisterously jovial heart and he agreed to drop us back at the headquarters. I could swear that it was sheer pity that had done the trick; for the so called magisterial power and authority of law which we embodied, had by then quite vanished from our wan and arid faces.

The very first wireless SITREP, dispatched by us from Donkamukam Police Station, that lay on the Deputy Commissioner's table at the district headquarters at Diphu the next morning read: "POLICE PATROLLING ON ALONG THE VVIP ROUTE STOP (.) NO UNTOWARD INCIDENT REPORTED FROM ANYWHERE STOP (.) SITUATION UNDER CONTROL AND CLOSE WATCH STOP (.) MSG ENDS STOP (.)"

(Hamren, Karbi Anglong, February 1993)

CLUELESS IN CHARCHIM

The crisis had blown over. We were all preparing to return home. People had already started moving back to their hearths and homes and everyday two to three relief camps were closing down on an average. The only major problem that we envisaged was the rehabilitation of those people who had crossed over from Karbi Anglong hills to the neighbouring plain district of Nagaon and those who had come over from the other hill district of North Cachar Hills in panic during the sudden ethnic upheaval between the Karbi and the Dimasa communities. Deep mistrust had impacted the psyche of the people, and it would take some time to heal. There was nothing we could do hasten the process. So we concentrated on the usual humdrum job of payment of ex-gratia to the next of kin of the dead and to those who were injured, distribution of GR (Gratuitous Relief) and RG (Rehabilitation Grant) and such other mundane peripheral stuff, knowing full well that these were mere temporary sops to get over the immediate crisis, and that time and time alone it was, that could heal the nasty scars which had cut through the souls of those affected; much like the balm applied to the burn injuries of the two orphaned children who were lying in the small hut of Mr Pator (a local press correspondent who had volunteered to take them in, in spite of his own many children), after being rescued from the deep jungle where they had fled in panic after watching their parents being shot in front of their eyes and their home go up in flames of racial hate.

Although simmering for quite some time back with sporadic incidents of killing and arson here and there, the whole thing had suddenly erupted with the mowing down of 21 innocent passengers of the two hapless Autonomous Council buses on the fateful morning of October 17, by some insurgent outfit. Disposal of heaps of bodies, post-mortems, mass cremations, opening of relief camps, deployment of paramilitary forces in vulnerable areas, night patrolling, medical camps and transmission of daily Situation Reports in Format I and II---The Grind….the relentless Grind. We had gone through it all as part of our routine magisterial job, and here we were at it yet once again. There was precious little else that we could do but hang in there and go through the dull drab heartless routine with all its déjà vu…just sit through the Grind and let time do the rest.

Ten days had passed and we had all put in tireless effort, sometimes working concertedly for eighteen to twenty hours at a stretch to put together the administrative machinery totally thrown out of gear, and set up some thirteen relief camps housing seven thousand plus displaced souls, aged people, pregnant women, nursing mothers and underfed children; and then as surely as the rainbow follows the rain NGOs started pouring in with their stock of relief materials, medicines and other goodies, flooding the relief camps. Well dressed people, beautiful faces with beautiful vehicles. And we like poor Eliot watched them *"Come and go; talking of Michael Angelo."*

But things were definitely beginning to improve. Peace initiatives had already been started both at the highest level by the political authorities as well as on the ground by local community groups to defuse the situation and rebuild the lost confidence between the two warring ethnic communities. Normalcy was returning fast.

Low down the rung, with the active cooperation of the District Council members, we too got busy to take the last initiative, which was to take the people of the bus carnage and arson-affected villages of *Charchim* and *Prisek* back to their homes, or rather, where they once used to be. But before that could be done, a fixed picket of paramilitary forces had to be stationed within the precincts of the village itself. And so, in spite of the heavy drag which was already weighing us down, we embarked on this Final Mission, to identify whatever ramshackle building that could be found nearby those forest villages for the purpose.

It was on our way there that I sighted him for the first time; neat, well-brushed and healthy, prancing sprightly up and down the spot where the bus carnage had occurred. He stopped for a while and glanced wistfully at the long line of cars as we passed him by. I looked back and saw him again resuming his restless prancing up and down the ill-fated stretch as if, looking for something----looking for someone. He was running round and round, sniffing here, sniffing there, as if he had picked up some strong familiar scent, but yet was unable to home in on the object of his search. He seemed to be highly agitated and frustrated. I saw him running round and round until the bend of the road cut off the line of vision.

Some two kilometers uphill we finally succeeded in identifying the ramshackle Public Works Department Inspection Bungalow where the paramilitary forces of the picket could be housed. The departmental officials accompanying me immediately got busy discussing the logistics. But much as I tried, I could not take my mind off the lovable well-groomed brown and furry dog, who was frantically searching for something or someone around the ill-fated stretch of the road downhill.

As we moved back on our return journey downhill, I grew more and more restless to reach that spot where I had spied him first. And as sure as I had thought, he was still there, moving up and down in a lithe graceful trot --- sniffing and searching. I asked the driver to slow down allowing the other vehicles to pass us by. I could see a line of shoes and ladies' slippers strewn all along the road. Pieces of broken windscreen glass lay scattered among the black lubricants and wooden ashes of the ill-fated bus, which had been removed by then. A light stench of blood still hung in the dank air around. How I wished I could help the poor lost dog in finding who or what he was looking for! I really wished I could explain to him what all had happened and why. Why all that massacre? Why all this hate? But how, for all the world, could I ever do that?... I was as much clueless as he.

(Kheroni, Karbi Anglong, October 2005)

THE THIRD WAVE

The whole town was under water. Hordes of people, cattle, straw, hand carts and torn bedding wraps, clothes and household utensils were lined up along the National Highway for long stretches throwing normal traffic completely out of gear. Unexpected heavy late September rain in the upper catchment areas of the mighty Brahmaputra had resulted in an unprecedented gush of tidal waters downstream which just swept away hutments, which had mushroomed in the scores of sandbars across the mighty river Brahmaputra, along with crops and cattle, in a massive bewildering flash. Most of the embankments which had provided shelter to the villages on the river bank had also given way before the gushing tide and people had no other option but to rush in a frenzied scurry for the nearest accessible highway. The Third Wave had struck.

The first wave of floods had come on in early June, followed by another in July which was more devastating. But thankfully it had ended after creating two weeks of utter havoc. Most of the displaced people were returning to their riverine villages with the bundles of tin roofing, which they had received as part of the Government rehabilitation grant, to construct their broken homes anew, which would hopefully see them through for yet another year. Engineers and Revenue officials were assessing the damage to roads and bridges and drawing up a plan for reconstruction, hoping to rebuild them over the next few months before the onset of the next year's monsoon. Schools and offices which had been converted to temporary relief shelters were hurriedly being cleared up. And with shops and markets opening up, life was gradually limping back to normalcy and soon it would all be business as usual yet once again. Looking at the mighty Brahmaputra, with its calm blue glistening waters, flowing majestically down to the distant sea, one could hardly imagine the calamitous havoc that it could at times wreak.

After a long and arduous spell of sleepless relief and rehabilitation duty for over a month Adarsh had taken two days leave. Being young recruits, he and his two other fellow executive magistrates had to bear the brunt of the field duties like requisitioning of boats and vehicles, accompanying the army personnel and the first response teams for rescue operations, evacuation of villages, opening and running of relief camps, procuring daily ration for the relief camp inmates and fodder for their cattle besides providing the bare essentials like utensils, blankets, clothes for the women and children, medicines and health care, drinking water and sanitation. Before the relief camps were opened they had even to pack and air drop food packets from air force helicopters in remote and inaccessible areas for the hundreds of marooned people taking shelter on the narrow embankment stretches or high grounds. He very vividly remembered the first day when the news of the first flash flood had come crackling in over the walkie-talkie of the Additional Superintendent of Police in the Deputy Commissioner's office chamber. They had to act fast. And so he had to hurry and ask the supply officials to pack whatever food stuff and water they could get hold of in the market and send them to the air force helipad some fifty-five kilometers away and load them during the night itself as the pilots intended to take off at the first visibility in the morning, given the prevailing cloudy weather conditions. Having laboriously collected the GPS coordinates from the huge map at the army camp, he had set off for the air force station in the night itself, so as to reach there latest by 04:00 hrs in the morning.

The heavy air force cargo chopper took off at 05:12 hrs sharp. After travelling for some twenty minutes or so they were hovering over the area which had been the worst hit, scouring the ground for some suitable place to land. But all they could see was a vast sea of flood waters dotted with half sunken house roofs and tree tops scattered here and there. The rest of the area was all covered with clouds and visibility was very low. After hovering around fruitlessly for some five minutes, the pilots were of the opinion that landing was impossible and there was no other option but to return to base and make another attempt sometime in the afternoon. Hundreds of human beings and cattle were starving down there, and Adarsh could not swallow the idea of just leaving them like that and turn away hoping for good weather. The despairing form of the frail old man, whom they had to abandon to his fate on that turbulent rocky creek, only because of intensely low visibility, on an earlier occasion, still pricked his conscience. Suddenly it came to his mind that there was a well-know mosque situated on a hill top somewhere in that area, popularly known as *Poa Macca*, because of the 250 grams of earth which some *Pir* had fetched way back from the holy city of Mecca and buried there to establish a mosque. Over the roaring sound of the rotor, he somehow shouted out and gestured to the co-pilot and convinced him to veer round and steer the chopper there and give it a try. With no definite coordinates available, it was like driving through the air with only eyesight for guidance. But fortunately soon enough, they could spy the hill and the mosque standing tall and majestic surrounded by a light fog at the base. The chopper homed in over the area, circling round and round looking for a fairly flat ground to land. After the fifth low and risky sortie, they could see a plateau-like natural helipad formation on a low neighboring hillock below, constructed there by providence itself, as if. The chopper managed to touch down safely. This time they had done it.

Anyway the ordeal was over now and he was back home shopping with his wife, buying some dresses for the children, and looking for a gift to present his wife on her birthday tomorrow. Two days leave was a luxury for people like him, who were expected to be twenty-four hours on duty, if not actually physically but mentally nonetheless. They spent the whole day shopping, picking up small inexpensive trifles which caught their fancy and returned after a late lunch at a popular Chinese food joint. The next day they would spend at home celebrating a quiet birthday with the family and close friends. Being somewhat tired and there being so much to talk and listen to the children that they did not care to listen to the news that evening and retired to bed early.

The phone rang at 11:55 at night. The Deputy Commissioner was on the line himself. There was a third wave. And this time the flood was so sudden and severe that everyone was caught unawares and there were unconfirmed reports of ten people dying at the very first blow. Adarsh was asked to cancel his leave and report for duty immediately by next morning. By the time he put down the phone it was 00:10 hrs. So he kissed his wife and wished her "Happy Birthday", and went back to bed. The Deputy Commissioner's voice had sounded intimate on the phone. He was not ordering, but rather pleading with him to come back fast. From the very first day he had taken a sort of liking for him. He was like a father figure as well as a friend; not only to him but to the other three new recruits, Anup, Zakir and Rita as well. He had literally taken them under his wing and endeavored to acquaint them with each and every nuance of the complex art of civil administration. He had been a sportsman once, and so, even at that advanced age he retained that natural gusto and the boyish élan. He would always tug them along to football matches and several hunting and fishing trips on holidays. Some of the routine monthly review meetings were held at scenic locales and picnic spots instead of stuffy conference halls. He would also chide them when they would embark on foolhardy missions, on their own, like tracking down rhino-horn and drug smugglers in the dead of night, without proper security or intimation. The near dead Officer' Club was revived under his patronage, and there were regular sessions of rummy, snooker and, of course tennis, of which he was an addict.

There was utter chaos in front of the Deputy Commissioner's office when he arrived at eight in the morning, driving down the seventy odd kilometers at break-neck speed from home. Displaced agitated people, women with half clad children trailing them, hand carts over laden with hurriedly packed bedding, clothes, corrugated roofing sheets, bamboo poles, utensils and other sundry household paraphernalia clogged all the approach roads. The entrance was choked with a motley crowd of political activists holding placards and shouting angry slogans. Security personnel were struggling to bring the situation under control. Parking the jeep somehow outside on the road itself, he elbowed his way through the horde of people, clambered up the stairs, and dashed for the Deputy Commissioner's chamber at the far end. A meeting was already in progress.

Officers from various departments were all present, all stiff-lipped and serious, conjecturing how best to cope with the unprecedented third wave of flood, and put the official machinery into gear yet once again.

The two preceding waves of flood had fortuitously been a sort of rehearsal for everyone present. They had done it before. It was just a matter of re-organizing their teams, get their acts together, and go all the hog over it yet once again. Only that this time round the scale of disaster was huge, and if weather forecasters proved true, the situation was likely to get worse over the next couple of days. While the overall tone of the meeting was starkly grave, with every one appreciating the gigantic scale of effort that was to be put in, some lighter moments could not be missed, like the one when the vulnerable-looking Additional Deputy Commissioner shot off a wireless message to the Officer-in-Charge of the local police station to apprehend the hapless rhino, which had been washed away from the Kaziranga wildlife sanctuary upstream, and was now creating havoc among the riverine villages on the sandbars dotting the vast deluge of the mighty Brahmaputra, now in its most devastative form.

While everyone was speaking of requisitioning of boats and vehicles, including the inflated rubber OBMs of the disaster management teams and the army, realizing the massive span of the disaster, Adarsh tentatively suggested something unusual, that of requisitioning the large inland water passenger vessels. They were the only ones with which one could attempt to take on the might of a river in full surge, he argued. While most were taken aback with this unconventional proposal, the Deputy Commissioner thought that it was right. He immediately instructed his deputy to sign the requisition forms, addressed to the concerned authorities, and hand them over to Adarsh so that he could requisition and bring them up from the jetty some ten miles across downstream, as the crow flies, where they were based. But it would take almost two hours to cover the seventy kilometers distance by road.

It was almost dark when Adarsh ultimately succeeded, after much cajoling, in convincing the inland water authorities to sanction one moderately large two-decked vessel. It took almost another two hours for the captain and the crew to assemble, then to re-fuel and load the provisions. When all was ready the captain suggested that they anchor for the night somewhere near the town and set off early in the morning when there would be better visibility. In doing so he and the crew could spend the night with their families. Adarsh too secretly felt tempted to do so. It would be a pleasant surprise for his wife to have him back home on her birthday. But he had earlier seen children and women clinging for their very lives to tree tops among the surging flood waters, which could anytime wash them away to oblivion. May be there was still someone clinging out there among the dark swirling waters, waiting to be rescued. So standing on the top deck of the requisitioned vessel and gripping the iron railing firmly he said a decisive no. The situation was grave and they could not afford to delay and would have to start immediately. They would travel through the night so as to reach their destination by early morning.

The progress upstream in the hazy moonlit was slow. The gushing waters moving frenziedly downstream drove a strong gale. Feeling somewhat uncomfortable Adarsh went down to the cabin of the captain. They had a hot cup of black tea together. The captain was an old hand and he had many a story to narrate. The night passed between dozing and conversation and soon it was day. It was 5:35 in the morning when they had finally docked on a bank along the national highway where the water was moderately deep, so as to avoid getting sand banked. Hopping off the long plank which they had laid across, Adarsh got into the nearest jeep available and sped off to the Deputy Commissioner's office.

The office was a flurry of activity. Officials and staff engaged in relief duty were hurrying past each other with bunch of papers in hand and every room was full of people presenting requisitions for provisions or vehicles, cash advances, bills of fuel, firewood and kerosene and what not. Clerks were bending over, scrutinizing papers and requisition slips and entering every transaction in their massive dog-eared registers. The Deputy Commissioner's chamber too was full of officials of different departments. They were all at a loss how to reach the foodstuff and fodder to the hundreds of people in the marooned villages. All roads being under waist deep water there was no way the jeeps or trucks could move. As most people were using their boats themselves, there were no boats left to be requisitioned. The few country boats which had been requisitioned earlier were grossly insufficient, and even these could not dare to venture out into the surging tidal waves of the river in spate. Now coming to know that the inland water vessel had arrived, they were all keen to pass on the bulk of their responsibilities to Adarsh. Finding no other way, Adarsh finally accepted the responsibility and asked them all to load all their provisions of food grain, fodder and medicine onto the vessel docked near the highway. He requested them to complete the loading latest by 3:00 pm in the afternoon, so that the vessel could move out into the swollen river well before sunset.

After finishing all other pending official formalities, he went back to his official quarter and hurriedly shoved his bare necessities of a towel, toothpaste & brush, a change of clothing, a pair each of sneakers and slippers into a backpack, put on his wind cheater and headed for the vessel, mentally prepared to embark upon a two day voyage, at the very least. He always loved water. So in spite of the onerous responsibility thrust upon him, he felt a secret inner thrill to be out there in the deep.

Arriving at the river bank alongside the highway at 3:00 pm sharp, where the ferry was docked, he was immensely disappointed to find that the loading was still going on. Only half the vessel was full with sacks of rice and other food grains. Officials of two other sectors were still unloading their trucks with a medley of on-the-spot hired laborers carrying huge sack-loads of grains and pulses on their bent backs across the gangway. The Veterinary officials were there too, with their huge truckload of fodder, but they had to wait for their turn, till the loading of the food grains were over. The Medical officials were nowhere to be seen. But they had sent word that they were already on their way and would be there soon. What worried Adarsh was the news that one of the Sector Officers was still awaiting for his trucks to arrive at the distribution godown. These had to be first unloaded at the godown, the stock docketed and re-issued, and then again loaded onto new trucks before they could be brought for unloading and loading on to the ferry. This would take two hours, at the very least, he calculated. It would already be dusk by 5:00 pm and it was uncertain if they could set sail in the dwindling twilight then. Anyway he asked everyone to hurry and making his way precariously along the gangway, went on to the ferry to take stock of the materials that had already been loaded and getting the requisite papers signed by the concerned officials present, indicating the quantity earmarked for each particular destination of the villages that lay scattered some ten to fifteen miles across the length and breadth of the wide swollen river.

A meeting was convened on the ferry itself where revenue officials, village heads and representatives of the concerned villages, who had earlier come on shore, were present. By the time all formalities were completed, it was already getting dark. The fodder trucks, which were still waiting, were given just half an hour's time to unload.

Just as the crew was readying to lift anchor, another two trucks arrived, one carrying the medicines and the other loaded with sacks of rice. The doctors and the para-medical staff insisted that it was vital to load the medicines too, and it would not be proper to leave them behind. The departure had, therefore, perforce to be delayed further. It was already dark by the time the loading of the medicines and the official formalities were over. The sky was dark with thick clouds, and only a nebulous ray of moonlight lit up a thin narrow portion of the sky. The truck laden with rice stood on the bank as it was. It would take almost an hour to unload it and there was no time to do so now. They would have to leave without wasting another minute, if they were to reach the mainstream safely; guided by whatever little visibility the filtered moonlight provided. But out on the bank a motley crowd of people suddenly gathered around the unloaded truck and started shouting slogans, demanding that that truck too should be unloaded and the rice bags be loaded on to the ferry. They would not allow the ferry to leave otherwise. Adarsh sniffed this to be the handiwork of the political agents of a section of the opposition party and other disgruntled elements and *agents provocateurs*. They were out there, right from the very beginning, to create mischief and spread discontentment among the flood-affected displaced immigrant population, who mostly populated the riverine and sandbar villages, to garner their support and show the government in a bad light. He had outwitted their game plan many times before and was in no mood to oblige them this time too. He, therefore, asked the relief officials who were there to take back the truck to the warehouse, and requested the captain and the crew to lift anchor and set sail. But the crowd refused to relent and grew more vociferous and aggressive at the decision.

In order to bring the situation under control, Adarsh called the leaders of the agitators onboard for a discussion to end the impasse. The captain of the ferry, the village heads and the other officials present were also invited to take part. The agitators argued that the *raison d'être* of the relief operation was to provide relief to the most needy. The food grains of the waiting truck were exclusively meant for the villages inhabited by impoverished immigrant people. If they were left behind, it would amount to a willful negligence, on the part of the Government, of the immigrant population of the state. Although the argument sounded apparently logical, its loud political overtone could hardly be missed by anyone present. The diabolic hint was that there was a strong suspicion that the huge quantity of food grains which were already loaded onto the ferry would be distributed solely among the local non-immigrant villagers and not to the immigrants. This was a downright travesty of truth, because as any sane mind can deduce, it is mostly the immigrants who, having no native village of their own, lived in sandbar villages situated along the course of the river. Who alone but they could be the beneficiaries? But this was no time to argue and queer the already surcharged political pitch. So Adarsh held himself back and invited the captain to express his opinion. The captain's view was terse. The ferry was already loaded to near full capacity of 9.5 tonnes. If it was loaded further, there was every chance of the vessel getting sand banked in the shallow waters, and then they would all have to wait another year for the next flood to come, to move out again. But cold technical indicators often get drowned before hot human impulsiveness. And so he finally suggested that the ferry would not move out during the night. They would wait for the next morning to watch the water level. If it did not go down, they would unload the food grains of the waiting truck onto the ferry and move out. If the water level fell, then they would have no other option but to leave back the unloaded truck and just go.

This impeccable logical suggestion of the captain should normally have left no scope for any further argument. But a section of the agitators were still dissatisfied and expressed the apprehension that this was only a ruse. When everyone would have gone back home, Adarsh and his team would quietly move out in the dead of the night, leaving the stranded truck behind with instructions to send it back to the depot. They said that they did not trust the administration at all. Adarsh had enough of it all. All through this while he had been uncharacteristically patient. But enough was enough. His head was heavy with two sleepless nights of frantic activity. The long dreary sailing upstream the previous night, the long day spent in running around, coordinating with some ten different departments and officials, racing against time to meet the deadline, had left his nerves uptight. He was hungry, thirsty and tired. He just could not take it any longer. There was enough of drama and now it was time to pack up. He called the security officer who was around, and ordered him to just clear the ferry of all outsiders and intruders. Mortified by watching the melodrama going on in front of their eyes for all this while, the paramilitary personnel were just waiting for the cue, as if. In one single swift concerted action they cleared the deck, literally, in a jiffy. Before their freewheeling wooden batons, rabble rousers, agitators, small-time politicians, upstart local leaders, self-styled social activists and their cronies, all scattered like straw and ran for cover, some literally falling head over heels into the water below.

Peace was restored. The situation was under control. There was a huge sense of relief all around. Adarsh too felt much better. At last he had performed his duty; done justice to the faith reposed on him as an Executive Magistrate, in stead of moving around like some hapless relief volunteer. He felt like being more true to himself and his calling; True to the mandate of the sacred *Gita*.

Now moving back to duty again, he summoned all the staff with the help of the captain and the crew. He ensured that all the relief materials were covered with plastic tarpaulins to protect them from the rain during the night. Realizing that it would be unsafe to let such a huge consignment of relief materials lying in the ferry throughout the night in such a volatile atmosphere, he sent a requisition to the police station and got a *posse* of armed police personnel to guard the ferry as well as the unloaded truck parked on the highway near the river bank. Having assigned the night duty to everyone, he asked the supply officials to help the crew in procuring the drums of diesel and refueling the vessel during the night itself so that they could set out early in the morning without wasting time for such sundry hassles. He requested the captain to keep the flood lights on, the whole night.

Having finished checking everything was in place, he now climbed down to the cabin below to have some grub with the captain, who was waiting for him, and catch a few winks on the narrow berth, if possible for the next two hours. The quiet meal shared with the captain was a pleasant surprise. There were three varieties of fish, one fried and two in curry. Seeing the surprised look in his eyes the captain explained that while the high drama was going on on the top deck, his men had been busy catching fish which were washed ashore in swarms by the flood. Adarsh felt most obliged by the captain's gesture. He was sorry that he had nothing to offer him in return. Suddenly he remembered that while the big fracas was going on in the evening, his fellow magistrate Anup had come onboard the ferry, just to see what was going on. He too was very busy with relief duties. But before leaving he whispered in his ear that he had left something for him in the cabin below. With all that hullabaloo going around during the day, he had quite forgotten about it.

He rushed back to his cabin and found a small gift-wrapped packet on the berth. He hurriedly opened the packet, curious to know what was inside. He smiled as he pulled out the pudgy dark bottle of rum. It was Old Monk, Anup's daily fare.

Anup and he, though batch mates, were apparently not the best of friends. Professional rivalry apart, Anup who was physically stronger, was often inclined to flaunt a bullying sort of attitude, in howsoever subtle a manner, which made Adarsh cringe sometimes. But paradoxically this and similar such traits of character was common to both of them. While the lanky and handsome Adarsh gave the impression of being more of a thinking sort of guy, right down there he was both mentally and physically quite violent, and this manifested itself in sudden bursts of irrepressible rage whenever anyone happened to show the slightest inkling of disrespect, insubordination or insipidity. Some of his rash actions had many a time left the entire administration red faced, leaving their boss, the poor Deputy Commissioner to reckon with mass protests, boycott and *bandhs* and other such unwarranted agitations through reconciliatory meetings, personal apology or hurriedly called press meets, to defuse the volatile situation. Anup, on the other hand, though an obvious bully both by built and look, was the most suave of persons in his public relation, the tone of his voice barely rising a note or two above whisper. But come the dark, he was a skunk of a guy, when one would actually find him in his true element. Dressed in his typical pair of faded jeans and a body hugging T Shirt, he could go on drinking like a fish and hog like a pig. He would shout at the top of his voice, utter the most obscene of expletives, breaking glasses, overturning tables, grabbing people by the collar, hitting them upfront in the face, and hurling the few hapless pacifiers who intervened, violently against the walls.

The captain, who was no stranger to alcohol by profession, was rather pleased with the unexpected lacing to their quiet dinner. Both he and Adarsh boisterously agreed that they indeed deserved the luxury of having a peg or two with the food after a night-long arduous sailing and a day of hectic haggling and frantic activity. It would definitely help calm their overstretched nerves and tired muscles. How thoughtful of Anup, Adarsh mused; the damned bugger did have some heart after all!

As they took generous bites of the spicy fish fry interspersed with swigs of the sweet liqueur, the conversation which started with bawdy jokes gradually veered towards literature. While Adarsh was throwing down his nuggets of soliloquies uttered within the vaults of the eerie turrets of the rotten state of Denmark or the sinister royal castles atop the hills of Dunsinane, all that the ferry captain, attempting to keep pace, could come up with was a misquoted " water

water everywhere…not a drop to drink." But with the muddy flood waters all around it was candidly down to earth and definitely the more contextually appropriate.

As the tête-à-tête was getting more stimulating, the dank waft of breeze coming in through the small cabin skylight abetted the effect of the warm liquor and soon the conversation was drifting into the realms of pure philosophy. Just as they were deliberating upon the Platonic concept of the democratic freedom of fools and asses moving shoulder to shoulder on the footpath, a home guard sentry popped his head between the half shut cabin door and said that there was a group of people gathered on the bank, who wanted to discuss something with the magistrate in charge. Adarsh got really very angry. The disruption was cataclysmic, no doubt about that. But it was not the sentry who irked Adarsh so much as the motley crowd which was still hanging around at that unearthly hour. Don't these people ever go to sleep? Won't they give the officials who are doing an honest job ever a break? Don't they ever tire of harassing people who are doing all they can within their capacity to bring things under control in order to give them some respite? It was past twelve in the night. They had argued with him the whole day till late evening; and they still had matters left to discuss! Adarsh just threw his arms up in despair. As he stood up abruptly and was about to rush out to confront them, the captain, who had seen more years than Adarsh, put a thick restraining hand upon his shoulders like an elder brother. He held him that way for a full minute and advised him to calm down and take it cool. Adarsh took a long deep breath, all the time looking at the floor; shook his head in assurance and went out.

As he was climbing up the steps to the upper deck, a strong gust of wind hit his face. He looked out over the vast expanse of the dark swirling waters, the ridges of the waves glittering past in the hazy moonlight. Involuntarily he held the railing and stood motionless for a while. Staring down at the waters, he saw the image of his wife Trishna standing in front of a vast endless ocean as if; the strong gale was trying its best to blow her away. But there she stood, brave and steadfast; withstanding the storm; her feet firmly planted on a rock, smiling at him reassuringly.

He quickly gathered himself up from the stupor and headed for the upper deck and asked them to put the plank down and allow only a few representatives to come over onboard to meet him. One of the four persons who came on board looked quite familiar; the same shabby beard; the same defiant look. Although he did not talk much, he definitely appeared to be the brain behind whatever game plan they were working at. The proposal they offered was that since the water was receding and there was very little possibility of loading the food grains onto the ferry from the unloaded truck parked on the bank, in the morning, the materials may as well be disposed of in the night itself by allowing the truck to be taken to a neighboring area where there were hundreds of marooned migrant people taking shelter but were not registered under any authorized relief camp. The local volunteers would do the distribution and submit the receipts later. Adarsh immediately had a hunch that this was some sort of a ploy, although he was not very clear as to what it actually was. The proposal, though apparently innocuous, was fraught with potential mischief, especially at night. Adarsh, therefore, told them plainly that whatever action that needs to be taken would be officially decided in the morning and not with some local volunteers at night. They went away angrily, blaming him of discrimination and partiality. It was already very late and Adarsh had a lot to do in the morning, which was just a couple of hours away. So he just ordered the guards to escort the visitors away from the deck and lift the plank. While being led away Adarsh could overhear them muttering threats of dire consequences. He just ignored them and headed for the cabin below. As he was climbing down the steps, he suddenly recalled where he had seen that bearded face. Yes, he had seen the man along with the group of people who had stormed the chamber of the Additional Deputy Commissioner along with the dissident local Member of Parliament who had raised his hand to strike the Additional Deputy Commissioner. Adarsh could not stand there as a silent spectator, so he had caught hold of the raised hand of the MP and pushed him back. "You don't know who I am!" the MP had thundered. "You don't know what I can do to you." "Your behaviour tells me who you are," Adarsh had retorted. "Do what you like, I don't care" he had added. A group, of army personnel who happened to be there at the moment somehow managed to disperse the crowd, with the MP too, slyly slipping out with his cronies, taking advantage of the melee which ensued, threatening of dire consequences. Adarsh had not paid much heed to what the MP had said at that time, but now he sniffed some serious mischief was at play.

The army personnel and Adarsh were natural buddies, as it were. There was a great deal of affinity between him and them both in attitude and temperament as well as the way they acted and thought. Gazing at the dark swirling waters, he fondly recalled the many escapades he had had with them during the earlier rescue operations, especially the one when he and a detachment of rowers had been marooned in the deep waters in the small army boat, when the outboard machine had suddenly gone dead throttled by the copious water hyacinth which floated all around. They had no option left but to bring out the wooden oars and paddle vigorously towards the faint glimmering lights visible on the distant shore. For full two hours they had rowed but only to find that they had been going round in circles, failing utterly to find a clear channel to advance towards the bank. With the army personnel grumbling that one could not work with so much of a risk, Adarsh had almost given up all hope when paradoxically the rescuers were ultimately rescued by one of the victims. A frail bare bodied immigrant, who was rowing by with all the belongings he could save, realized their predicament and swung a lantern of hope at them. There was no conversation, only an exchange of signals, such that are transmitted in the face of grave danger or crisis; just gestures between the rescuer and the rescued; a silent yet momentous communication of life reaching out to life. Following the flickering wisp of the hand held hurricane lamp, they somehow managed to reach an edge of the river bank, which was some four kilometers downstream from the destination they were purportedly heading for. Scrambling thankfully onto the land, they looked out in vain for the boatman to thank and reward him for saving their lives. But he had vanished as mysteriously as he had appeared….

Adarsh quickly finished his ad hoc dinner, wished the ferry captain goodnight and went off to his cabin berth to catch a few winks if he could before it was morning. But before that he ran up to the upper deck to see that all was okay and to instruct the police personnel on duty to keep a close watch.

Hardly an hour must have passed, when Adarsh was awakened from deep slumber with the sound of a clamour outside. Jumping out of bed in a jiffy, he fumbled up the steps on to the upper deck to find a large group of people gathered on the bank along the highway. The sentries informed that the unloaded truck which was parked on the road was gone. He quickly ordered the plank to be laid and rushed down from the ferry onto the road only to be harangued by a group of irate mob, who demanded to know from him where did he send the truck away. Some even went to the extent of accusing him of clandestinely sending the truck away with the purpose of selling the relief commodities to black-marketers. Adarsh was totally stunned by this strange and concerted accusation. He wondered who could have set a mischief afoot. He sternly asked the guards what had happened. They abashedly confessed that they had gone up onto the ferry to rest for sometime, as it was uncomfortable standing there for so long on the open road. Someone must have taken advantage of their short absence and taken the truck away, they said. But what about the driver, he asked. How could he have just left like that without any permission? He must have been forced by someone or made to connive, they casually conjectured.

Adarsh just did not know how to respond to such abject insipidity. He would have to deal with it later, he reckoned. Right now what was important was to locate the whereabouts of the truck and find out who had done such an atrocious act. He looked at his watch. It was 1:25 am and it was still dark. There was not a single official or policeman beside him as Adarsh stood his ground all alone, confronting single-handedly a much agitated and hostile crowd. He angrily reprimanded them all and asked them what they were all doing when the truck was moving away right in front of their eyes. Why didn't they stop it from going if they had such strong suspicions? They could have caught hold of the driver red-handed and detained the truck themselves and then confronted him. Why did they keep standing there as mute spectators, doing nothing then, and now coming up with wild allegations against him? Why didn't they shout then as they were doing now? The crowd all fell mute and stepped back unable to confront the candid burst of truth. It was strange, really very strange! With that entire milling crowd around, there was not a single person who could provide him a clue, except for a few murmurs from some that they saw the truck going up the road away towards the East. Adarsh just did not know what to do. There was not a vehicle with him to move or give chase as he had sent them all back, thinking he would not need them as he would be moving out in the ferry in the morning. As he stood wondering, a police patrol jeep came speeding down from the East, the direction in which the truck had reportedly gone. Adarsh immediately intercepted the jeep and asked the police party whether they had seen any truck passing them by. They said no. They had been on duty along the track for the last three hours or so but they had not seen a single loaded truck pass that way. Adarsh quickly got on to the jeep and asked them to head for the police station. Before leaving he again ordered the guards to be alert and not to allow any outsider to board the ferry.

The police station was all empty except for the lone 'duty' who was dozing crouching on a chair in the corner. He woke up with a start and gave a limp salute as Adarsh nudged his shoulders and asked him to call the Officer-in-Charge. As the 'duty' hurriedly went away to call the OC, Adarsh sat there, still wondering whether it was not a part of some big conspiracy hatched by the wily MP with whom he had had a tiff in the room of the Additional Deputy Commissioner, in the morning. But he had very little time in his hand and had to sort things out as soon as possible as he had to leave with the ferry at the strike of dawn. They had wasted the whole of last evening unloading and loading.

There were hundreds marooned out there, starving on the flooded sandbars, waiting eagerly for the relief he was to carry. He did not know how it was all going work out now. Although it was untimely, he made bold and called up the Deputy Commissioner and informed him about all what had happened and how a group of people suddenly gathered and had heckled him, throwing all sorts of wild allegations at him and the administration about the missing truck. He requested the Deputy Commissioner to depute some other officer for the ferry duty and allow him to go after the case of the missing truck as he had a strong hunch that there was some sort of deep conspiracy behind it all, and that he was sure, he would be able to unravel it before daybreak. He assured him that if he was allowed a free hand, he would soon get to the bottom of the plot and be able apprehend the culprits and recover the missing truck along with the relief materials. But it seemed that the Deputy Commissioner clearly did not appreciate the stinging urgency of the situation or be able to sniff this to be a part of a greater game plan. He sounded totally unperturbed over the phone. He merely asked him to inform the police and tell them to look for the missing truck and go back home. Adarsh was totally mortified then, but later when he understood why he had said so; it was much too very late.

The OC came in bleary-eyed but in full uniform. He was surprised with all what Adarsh had to say. He immediately called out the reserve force and soon they all landed up at the place of occurrence on the highway near which the ferry lay anchored. There was a quick inspection of the spot followed by questioning of the bystanders, whose number had remarkably dwindled by then. The finding was the same. Someone had seen the truck move away towards the East, others said that it had reversed and parked on the other side.

But they all sounded vague and confused. There was not a single person who could give a definite answer. The OC reasoned that there was only one direction the truck could have gone i.e. towards the East. The Highway ran from West to East. Had it gone the other way it would have had to pass through the town and someone would have definitely noticed. Besides the police station was only half a kilometer back. The policemen doing night duty would hardly allow any loaded truck to go past without paying a legitimate or illegitimate levy.

There was no point delaying there any further, and so it was decided that the OC go off with an armed posse towards the East to give the truck a chase as it could not have gone far, given the load it was carrying. Adarsh got down from the jeep at the spot where the incident had occurred and volunteered to stay on there, to ensure that no further incident took place, and to make further enquiries from the motley group of hangers on.

There was no crowd there to heckle him this time round. So Adarsh went very close to a small group of bystanders who were whispering something among themselves. They all fell silent as he approached. They averted their glance as he looked at each of them in the eye. Finally he physically caught hold of one of the more simple looking ones, put an arm around his shoulders and took him aside cajoling him to speak up without fear. He wouldn't divulge anything he promised. The man looked about nervously. "Sir, you are a very good man I know. It's…it's all a plan of the…" The man was just opening up when three or four of the bystanders approached and shouted him down. "What, what nonsense are you talking? When you haven't seen or don't know anything, don't speak like a fool. Sir, he is a stupid fellow who does not know anything. We were all asleep and we haven't seen anything." They literally pulled the man out of Adarsh's fold and rebuked him sharply. "Go…go and sleep with your wife and children and don't speak nonsense…" An abrupt silence followed, and the group melted away one by one into the dark.

They had snooped down and snatched the vital clue from him. Adarsh stood alone and motionless, staring down hard at the wide dark road that winded away in front of him like some monstrous black inert python, its pitch black surface glistening ominously under the clouded mid-night moon.

Having nothing else left to do at the moment, Adarsh climbed back on to the ferry to ensure that all the loaded foodstuff was intact and no one had tampered with them while he was away. Everything was intact. He pulled a small stool and involuntarily sat down and waited, thinking against thought itself.

He must have sat that way for more than a full one and half hours before the OC returned. "Didn't find a damned clue", he said. "Made several enquiries, there are crowds of people down there taking shelter all along the highway. None of the buggers would open their mouths! Strange…really very strange! I must say." Adarsh was silent. Listening less and thinking more. How could this happen? The huge truck laden with sacks full of rice, passing along the single highway at that hour of the night when there was hardly any traffic and no one had seen anything! How could that be possible? Surely there was something behind it all. Why were the people not speaking up? Were they afraid of something; Or of someone? Was there a well coordinated conspiracy or something? Whatever it be, some downright reckless brain was undoubtedly at work somewhere behind the scene. Adarsh tried desperately to think who could be behind all this mischief. He scoured the deep recesses of his mind trying to recall the face of that someone who could have such a deep-rooted animosity against him to go to the extent of embarking on such a reckless misadventure fraught with dangerous consequences. A plethora of incidents raced through his mind in a couple of nano seconds. It suddenly dawned upon him that his style of dealing with situations and persons with daring élan had created a host of secret enemies who could have now joined minds to put him into such a predicament. But it was not this alone. The political scenario too was extremely volatile. What with the sense of acute vulnerability throbbing in the minds of hordes of the immigrant population, of being detected and deported as foreigners, with the coming of the new government in the state, riding on the raging tide of anti-foreigner sentiment of the ethnic local populace! There was deep conspiracy somewhere out there; no doubt about that. There could have been elements who were planning his discomfiture. But more than that there was a silent dark political hand which was at work to embarrass the Government and show it in a bad light before the nation and the world. A government which was ruthless and violative of the human rights of the minorities!

Adarsh suddenly shook himself out of his stupor. This was not the time to surmise and ponder. It was a time to think quickly and take appropriate fire-fighting measures. He quickly rose and instructed the officials and the policemen there to be alert and guard the relief materials loaded on the vessel so that no further mischief could be done and left along with the OC in his jeep. At the first turning he got down and headed straight for the Deputy Commissioner's Bungalow, while the OC carried on to the police station. He looked at his watch. It was 5:42 am.

The Deputy Commissioner was already up. He was sitting on the balcony of the old wooden bungalow in his spotless white pajamas drooping over his first cup of morning tea. He saw Adarsh walking up the narrow pathway across the sprawling lawn below, but displayed no reaction at all, sitting with his typical droop on the elongated cane easy chair. But as Adarsh came within earshot he muttered something and waved to him to come straight up. As Adarsh wished 'Good Morning Sir', he asked him to pull up a chair. Adarsh blurted out the whole story in one breath and suggested that it was necessary to act fast as he suspected that there was some deep conspiracy behind the whole episode. The Deputy Commissioner seemed totally unperturbed. He just looked at him closely and said "You're looking too overworked and tired. Just go to the guest room, have a good wash and try and get some sleep. Don't worry I will handle this. There's a set of spare pajamas and slippers there. You can use those."

The shower was greatly refreshing, and after two restless sleepless nights Adarsh just sank into the mattress and before he knew it, was drawn into a deep slumber.

He remained that way for some full eight hours or so when he was suddenly awakened by sounds of some commotion outside; some sound of many people shouting together. Gradually he could decipher that they were raising some sort of slogans out there. He leapt out of the bed and rushed out to the open balcony. Sure enough! Exactly as he had guessed! A large procession, consisting of an overwhelming number of immigrant people, carrying placards had gathered at the gate of the Deputy Commissioner's Bungalow. They were shouting full-throated slogans decrying him, the Deputy Commissioner, the local Legislator, the ruling party and the Government. While he was sleeping, they had got themselves organized and had hatched a nefarious plan to embarrass the Government and the ruling party. He had warned the Deputy Commissioner in the morning, but he had not given it any importance and had just brushed aside his apprehensions as figments of a tired overworked mind. The incident of the missing truck was not a case of common theft which was best left to the police to investigate. It was a part of a larger, much larger game plan. He later came to know from the Superintendent of Police that the dissident Member of Parliament and the local dissident Legislator of the ruling party had got together with the leaders of the Opposition Party and convened a meeting at the Circuit House wherein they had hatched the entire game plan. They had also lodged an FIR against him with the local police station, alleging that he had conspired with some local ruling party workers and stolen the truck load of rice and sold it the local black-market.

Not aware of any such thing then, he rushed down to meet the Deputy Commissioner in his Bungalow Office below. Although he found him to be a little worried now, he realized that he was not fully seized of the matter and the huge ramifications it would have were it not nipped in the bud right there and then, by arresting the leaders who were playing upon the raw sentiments of a large group of flood-stricken susceptible immigrant population. The sense of vulnerability was two-fold. One that they were immigrants smarting under the fear of being detected and deported on suspicion of being illegal migrants form the neighboring country of Bangladesh, and the other that they were rendered homeless now, their make-shift habitations on the periodic sandbars inundated by the mighty Brahmaputra which seemed hell-bent upon reclaiming what was its own, and in no hurry to recede or relent. The Deputy Commissioner was no politician but a straight forward bureaucrat. He saw the entire episode of the missing truck as nothing more than another police case of ordinary theft. Being appointed by the ruling party which had come to power riding upon the crest of a state-wide tidal wave of sub-nationalism directed against illegal migrants, he could hardly imagine that a motley group of immigrant people could do any harm to him or the Government. A simple and straight police action and the whole thing would peter out in a second, he must have guessed. "Let them agitate for sometime. They are already a half-starved lot. Soon they will all be tired and go home" he said; now sipping his evening cup of tea. "Just keep a close watch" he instructed the Officer-in-Charge of the Headquarter police station who had come to brief him about the deteriorating situation and seek instructions to act. "If they just want to shout slogans for sometime, let them do it. It would help ease some of their pent up frustrations, after all. Then let them go home. If they try to cross the *Lakshman-rekha* just round up some of the smarter ones, and the rest will automatically disperse and go back home." "Right Sir", the officer said saluting and rose to go. They exchanged a quick knowing smile before he left. Both the Deputy Commissioner and the police officer were old hands at handling far more difficult law and order situations. This was just another routine stuff. "Happy now?" the Deputy Commissioner said, winking at Adarsh who had been sitting mortified all through the insensitive conversation. "You must be feeling quite hungry. Come let's see what they have cooked up for dinner."

Adarsh hardly had any appetite. He found it hard to swallow the logic of the Deputy Commissioner. Though inexperienced as an administrator, he had been in politics all through his student life. He knew what sort of mischief political activists are capable of; the havoc that they can wreak, once they can entice a gullible mob into their trust for pushing their secret agenda by sugar-coating it in the garb of public interest. He tried his best to reason with the Deputy Commissioner through small talk across the dinner table but failed to make any dent. The night was a sleepless one.

As Adarsh sat bleary-eyed on the balcony in the morning he wondered why the Deputy Commissioner was keeping him in his house and not allowing him to go. He rued at the precious time that they were letting go by, doing nothing to address the situation as was called for. He had an uncanny apprehension of some great foreboding disaster lurking round the corner.

The day witnessed quite a number of visitors coming to meet the Deputy Commissioner; politicians, police officers, social activists, student leaders, unemployed youth leaders, women's group et al, as they come. No sooner one went out, another came in. At times there were three or four groups there together at a time. A great deal of hectic discussions were on, it seemed. The Deputy Commissioner had not cared to listen, and now he naturally had his hands too full to contain the situation. Not being able to resist himself any longer, Adarsh had gate crashed into one of the meetings, to find out what the hell was going on down there. He was promptly asked to leave and go and relax upstairs. Relax? When they were blundering from one wrong decision to the other? That things were gradually going out of control was obvious from the fact that a motley group of curious bystanders were thronging at the main gate of the Bungalow. So he decided to go out on his own without informing the Deputy Commissioner. As he came down and stepped onto the lawn, a blue jeep zoomed in through the gates. In stead of going to the parking in front of the Bungalow office, where all activity was going on it veered towards him and came to a sharp halt right in front of him. Out stepped Ajay his fellow magistrate and batch mate. Ajay took him aside and spoke to him in a strange urgent tone. It was obvious that Ajay knew as much as Adarsh was in the dark about what all was actually going on out there. "Do you have any luggage with you?" Ajay asked briskly. "No. I am in this dress for the last two days, but why are you asking me this?" "Look" said Ajay, "there's no time to lose. Just get onto my jeep and I'll drop you off at Tezpur. Now its 5 O'clock and we should be there by eight if we go at a speed. From there you can take a night bus and go to your home at Guwahati. Come on, let's leave." Adarsh was aghast at the proposal. "Why for the sake of God should I do that? Am I escaping or something like that? Why should I do so? Should I cow down like that to some mischief mongers who have gathered some ignorant people to shout slogans against me? Should I run away from some bunch of goons who have ganged up against me and the administration? What are all this police force and the Deputy Commissioner for? Can't they control the situation and bring the culprits to book?" "Adarsh you don't know, everyone is against you. No one is willing to help you at this time. Believe me. Come hurry!" "Thank you Ajay" Adarsh said. "You know I'm not someone like that. I don't run away from situations. I face them. Why should I be afraid of anyone when I have done nothing wrong? Why should I run away like a thief?" "OK, if that's your decision stay on. But I feel you should leave. All those crooks have ganged up against you. They have cooked up an FIR against you. They are taking advantage of the situation to get back at you for your tough action against them before." But Adarsh would not flinch against any threats and that too from crooks who he had booked earlier on for their misdeeds. "Ok then" Ajay said "I wish you all luck. I have to leave. Situation is very tense. We are all under attack. Even my movements are being watched. I'm going then. Good luck". Adarsh watched Ajay go out the main gate in his jeep without caring to meet the Deputy Commissioner, which he would never have done normally. In fact, he was one who would never miss an opportunity to curry favor with the Deputy Commissioner even at the cost of Adarsh or any of their other colleagues, for that matter.

Adash suddenly got an inkling that things were going from bad to worse. The conspirators had got the upper hand and that the Deputy Commissioner or the Superintendant of Police would perhaps not be able to contain the situation for much longer. The entire administration was on the verge of collapse. And the saddest part was that he himself, who had always been in the forefront of every crisis, was now not allowed to act, being a hostage for two full days in the Deputy Commissioner's Bungalow.

As twilight was setting in, Adarsh noticed a white car followed by a jeep, enter the campus. From the red flashing top light he could guess that it was the Superintendent of Police Mr Baruah. After some fifteen minutes or so the orderly came and said that the Deputy Commissioner had asked him to come over to the Bungalow office. As Adarsh hurriedly came down the wooden staircase and entered the office he saw the Deputy Commissioner and the Superintendent of Police talking in hushed tones. The Additional Deputy Commissioner, the one who had ordered the police instead of the forest officials to look out for the errant rhino the previous day, was also present. They all suddenly fell silent as he entered. The Deputy Commissioner looked up, smiled and gestured to him to take a seat. "We're in a big problem it seems" he said softly. His otherwise confident look was missing. His face looked withdrawn and wan and his eyes bore a distant forlorn look as if he was pondering upon something very deep and trying to find an answer which was evading him. An eerie uncomfortable silence followed. Everyone just looked at one another but no one spoke. "See" the Deputy Commissioner said breaking the uneasy silence, "the situation is not good at all. The Leader of the Opposition has come to Dispur from Delhi to make a first hand study of the flood situation in the state. He has already had had a talk with the Chief Minister today and he is very likely to visit our district tomorrow. The disgruntled politicians have somehow managed to include our district in his itinerary. We have to somehow put an immediate stop to this silly agitation going on here. Else they will have one more stick to thrash us with, and put the Government in a spot. What with the big contingent of the not-so-friendly national media which has come with him. They will flash the news all over the country in blaring headlines that the state Government is out to persecute the flood-stricken indigent immigrant minority people by depriving them of any relief during their time of distress." "Then Sir," Adarsh ventured, "we shouldn't waste any time and act immediately. Why are we not rounding up the rabble-rousers? The leaders I mean. They are acting in the most reprehensible manner and misleading these ignorant poor homeless people." "We can't afford to do this now", the Superintendent said very wisely. "Had we acted earlier we could have brought the whole thing under control in no time. But we have allowed the matter to drift for two long days. If we act tough now, the blame would be doubled. First, that the administration had neglected the poor minority people, and secondly that now we are beating up these hungry homeless who have come on to the streets to protest against the injustice meted out to them. We would not have any place to hide." The Superintendent of Police had a solid point and no one could deny that. "But Sir," Adarsh interjected, "the whole issue here is regarding the missing or stealing of a single relief truck. I have already lodged an FIR with the police at midnight, and they are already investigating into the matter. What is this talk now of minorities being deprived or persecuted by the Government?" "You are very right", the Superintendent of Police said, but that was the scene yesterday, not today. They have manipulated the whole thing and converted it to a larger issue which cannot be handled by mere law and order methods. The whole thing has now become political and spun out of our grip. All we can do now is to show some action by which the situation can be defused." "And what is that?" Adarsh asked. "Look", the Deputy Commissioner said looking uncharacteristically apologetic. "We have worked out a plan. You go with the Superintendent to the police station. We will say that we have taken you there for some interrogation." Adarsh was aghast. He could not believe his ears. The Deputy Commissioner who had prevented him from taking any action on the spot, asking him to just inform the police and go to sleep and not to worry at all, saying something like that now!

"Look, this is just a show. We will have to put up an act as if we are taking some action. Go there, sit and have a cup of tea and chat for some time and come away. That's it. The crowd will have been pacified by then. And then you can coolly go home and rest. The rest we will handle. Don't worry, we're there. Nothing's going to happen to you." Adarsh just did not have any words to say, but just looked on. "I think that would be enough?" the Deputy Commissioner asked the Superintendent. "Yes Sir, I think that would suffice." Adarsh got into the Superintendent's car and they whizzed away out the main gate, meandering through the milling crowds in the street, and headed straight for the police station.

For someone who is unaccustomed the first sight of the insides of a police station is unnerving. Heaps of files piled up on the desks and still more moth-eaten ones stacked untidily on the dusty cobwebbed upper shelves, the list of wanted criminals, the crime chart boldly displaying the number of murders, rapes, thefts and other crimes committed during the month, the thick foreboding iron cross-bars of the lock-up gate, the pairs of handcuffs dangling from the board, a bunch of shady characters, with roped hands, huddled together on a creaky bench, do indeed present a veritable awful sight. But being an Executive Magistrate these were Adarsh's daily cup of tea. The police station was like his second home, as if. How so very often had he sat there gossiping and joking with those men in smart khaki uniforms during those long unending law and order duties! How many times had he rushed in there, walkie-talkie in hand, to transmit some urgent SITREP over the radio or to get transcripts of some intercepted messages of insurgents planning a bomb attack or some deadly ambush! He felt as if he was there on some normal duty to write some inquest report or something, quite unaware of the fact that the roles were reversed this time round. He was there to face interrogation, not to conduct one.

As he pulled up a chair and sat on it majestically he realized that there was an inexplicable silence all around. The uniformed guys who were all the time so noisy and boisterous were behaving in a strange manner with him. They were extra polite and made all out efforts to make him feel comfortable; responding to his friendly tête-à-têtes with unbefitting obsequious smiles. The Superintendent of Police, who had entered with him, had suddenly vanished from the scene. The Officer-in-Charge, who was beating up some poor howling suspect in the backroom, came sweating in from the door and took his seat opposite Adarsh. He too smiled at Adarsh in a strange manner and asked "What will you have Sir, Tea or Coffee?" Adarsh was flabbergasted. "Tea or Coffee alright, but why have you'll called me here for? The Superintendent and the Deputy Commissioner had said that you wanted to ask me something. Come on let's get on with it and finish that first." "Okay, okay…Sir" the OC replied. "We'll be doing that….there's no hurry…we have a lot of time in hand. Have the coffee Sir and relax. You're quite safe here. Don't worry." Adarsh was genuinely puzzled with this remark. "What are you talking about? I don't need any tea or coffee, thank you. Just ask what you have to ask, I'll just answer and leave." "You can't do that Sir. We can't let you go outside Sir. It is not safe. The instruction is that we must look after you and not let any one come in here to trouble or hurt you." Adarsh was at his wit's end. "What hurt or trouble are you talking about? Who will hurt me? What is all this nonsense about? Come give me the phone, I want to talk to the Deputy Commissioner." "As you wish Sir" he said handing over the phone. Adarsh dialed the Deputy Commissioner's number and waited impatiently for some one to pick up. The Personal Secretary picked up. "Hello! Deputy Commissioner's Bungalow… Who's calling please?" "I'm magistrate Adarsh speaking; please connect me to the Deputy Commissioner immediately. I've something very urgent to tell him." "OK Sir…just hold for a second…I'm connecting you to him." Adarsh waited with baited breath to hear the voice at the other end. Seconds passed as if they were hours. Finally the fragile voice of the Deputy Commissioner floated across. "Yes Adarsh, any problem? I hope everything's fine." "Fine…? Sir, they are saying that

I cannot go; that they have instructions to keep me here. I really don't understand what's going on. Why do I have to stay here the night long, in the police station? What is it all about? You said that they would ask me a few questions and that was all. It was just a show to appease the agitating crowds. They haven't asked me a single question and now they are saying that I cannot go and have to stay. I had told you last night itself that there was some big conspiracy behind all this. They have all…." The Deputy Commissioner cut him short. "Look Adarsh, this is not the time to discuss these matters. They have been asked to keep you there for the night. It is for your own protection. We'll talk about it later." "But Sir, this is just…." The Deputy Commissioner had already hung up.

As Adarsh instinctively put back the receiver in its hold he looked up blankly at the Officer-in-Charge, who was all this while following the conversation very intensely. "Sir, I had already told you to just sit back and relax. They have all abandoned you and are not going to do anything for you. They just do not have the guts. Please don't mind my saying so, but I have seen more years than you. I have encountered many such bastards during my long tenure of service. All these senior officials and administrators, my bare foot! They are all downright cowards; every one of them. All they can do is act high and mighty in front of people who are weak and helpless. Before the strong and mighty they are like purring kittens. Whenever a difficult situation arises they always push the juniors up to bear the brunt. If they struggle and manage to come out successful their seniors along with everyone up the ladder take the credit. If they happen to fail…. why? The blame can always be heaped upon them for a song. Sir, I have watched the dash and boldness you bring to your work. In fact, you remind me of my younger days, and I have taken a liking for you. Sir, what you need right now is a good lawyer. Just tell me whom do you trust, and I'll bring him to you in the morning". The scattered pieces were all falling in place now. Adarsh could now clearly see through it all. The talk of interrogation was a big flat farce. He was literally now under arrest. This is what they had done to pacify the agitating mob and their political bosses. That is why the Officer-in-Charge was talking of a lawyer; a lawyer to get him out on bail.

Adarsh did not have any stomach for dinner. He fell abruptly silent as if lost in a forlorn world which he had never known. He quietly slumped into the folding cot which they had laid out for him below the dirty wooden racks. He drank a glass of water and pulled the blanket over.

It was about 7:30 when he suddenly woke up hearing a heavy thud. Some of the cops had carried a bulky square bundle and dropped it heavily on the floor. A small pick-up van was sputtering outside. Must be some smuggled narcotic grass, which they have seized during the night; Adarsh thought. Instinctively he got curious and was about to ask what it was. But then suddenly realizing the circumstances he was in, he pulled himself back. Let them do what they like. Let them go to hell! Let the whole state go to the dogs! He couldn't care less for such things anymore. Let them handle it as they have been doing all along. May be they would take a lot of bribe and let the real culprit go. That is how things were. That is how they would always be.

A people get the sort of administration they deserve. So be it. He had other weightier things to worry about. He had himself to worry about. He thought of his wife and children. He despaired to think how they would react when they came to know that he had been arrested. What face would he have to show them? How would he explain? Suddenly he recalled the swift ephemeral vision of his wife with that distant look in her eyes which he had seen reflected in the swirling waters as he was climbing up the steps of the ferry the night before. She was trying to say something to him, as if. Was it a sign of warning? Was it her caring spirit which had flown down to communicate something to him, when she was fast asleep far away?

Two plates of breakfast were laid on the table; one for him and the other for the Officer-in-charge who now came in through the front door, looking fresh, well kempt and smart in his khaki starred uniform. "Come on! Let's have something to eat. I think we have a long day ahead." Adarsh forced a smile and said that he did not have an appetite. He would join him, nonetheless and have a cup of black tea and a biscuit. "As you wish; but I would advise you to have a good breakfast. I'm not sure we'll have time enough to pick some grub later on".

"Good Morning, Everybody"! It was Advocate Sharma at the doorway. The Officer-in-Charge must have called him up last night, Adarsh guessed. He was talking about getting some lawyer to plead for him. But was it really necessary? Adarsh was hesitant. "Good morning Mr Sharma! Come sit. Magistrate Adarsh has something very urgent to discuss with you." Adarsh was flabbergasted by this blunt intrusive concern. But that is a policeman's way of handling things. Without going into the nitty-gritty of issues, without caring about opinions and sentiments their main concern is how to handle the situation which is before them. If someone is sick what he needs is a doctor; if someone has a case against him he needs a lawyer, that's that. No beating around the bush; no dilly-dallying; no idle rationalization; but straight and simple solution vis-à-vis the problem. Adarsh had never asked for a lawyer in the first place, but faced with a *fait accompli*, he faltered "I....I...yes there's this...." Without making much ado the Officer-in-charge barged in "Let's not beat round the bush. Now Mr. Sharma, our friend Magistrate Adarsh here has been arrested. He wants you to move his bail petition before the Court." Although he had dimly guessed the situation he was in, Adarsh felt as if hit by a bolt at the sudden utterance of such explicit and unadulterated truth. The huge ramifications of the event now began to sink down upon him. He lost grip of his characteristic self-confidence and began to mentally grope for support. Mr. Sharma was an old regular at the Officer's Club. The Deputy Commissioner had first introduced him to Adarsh during a rummy game. From then on, if not friendship, a sort of peripheral bonhomie had built up between the two of them. They had shared quite a number of common escapades during the last two years or so even beyond the activities of the Club. Even professionally they seemed to share common vibes. That was the reason why Adarsh was feeling somewhat awkward and hesitant to take him in as his lawyer. The nascent camaraderie would be shattered once the relationship changed into that of client and lawyer. Anyway one can't just wish away harsh realities and so he ventured "Mr. Sharma I am really embarrassed, but they say that I would require a bail. Would you mind moving a bail petition on my behalf, if necessary?" "What 'if necessary'?" the Officer-in-Charge barged in again, as blunt as ever. "Of course, he has to move a bail petition for you, unless you don't want to go and stay in the jail." Another jolt hit Adarsh; a very hard one this time. Case, arrest, bail and now the jail! What was happening? Where had all his fellow magistrates and the seniors gone? Where had they all vanished? Was there no one who could do something about it all? Had the entire administration collapsed all together? What was happening? Where had all the powerful administrative fraternity, Executive Magistrates, Judicial Magistrates, Sub-Divisional Magistrates, Additional Deputy Commissioners and the Deputy Commissioner et al, all disappeared? Where were they all absconding? Why was he left to fend for himself all alone in this way? If anyone had raised a finger against him it was a challenge thrown against the whole administration. Why were they then not fighting it out together? Why was the all-powerful local Legislator for whom he had undertaken the greatest of risks not speaking up in his defense now? It was as if all walls were caving in one after the other, from his own stature as a magistrate to the Deputy Commissioner's guardianship and now even the police protection itself. The swift wand of time reducing him from the lofty position of a magistrate to that of a hapless hounded criminal, cajoling some lawyer, who was wont to pleading before him, to defend him in court now!

Anyway facts are facts. However harsh they might be they have to be always faced that way. He was all alone and there was none he could turn to for help or solace. He wondered if anyone had informed his wife and family about all this by now. He himself would never do that for sure. How would he be able to explain to them all what had happened? How would he able to convince his wife that he was innocent? How could he dare face her in this condition? What would he have to say? How would his old mother and in-laws take it? His children were too very young to be shocked that way! Come what may, he decided that he would never let any of them know anything. They would be producing him before the magistrate in the afternoon. He would himself pray for bail on personal bond.

It was at about 2 o'clock in the afternoon when they lined up the jeeps that were to escort him to the court. It was hot and the air full of dust. A curious mob of sundry people were gathered around the police station consisting of predominantly flood-affected immigrants from the neighbouring riverine areas for whose rescue and relief he had been giving his all. Interspersed among them was a motley group of *agents provo'ca'teurs* who were raising hostile slogans against the administration and the government and pushing the crowd forward, egging them on to agitate. A company of additional para-military forces had to be deployed to keep the multitude at bay, to make way for the jeeps to move forward. The shouting and clamor continued all the way right up to the very door of the Chief Judicial Magistrate's court room.

As he stepped out of the jeep with a bunch of policemen huddling around him, his eyes fell on the familiar figure of a woman waiting distraught yet silent and stoic among the milling crowd. As she turned hearing the noise their eyes met and held that way for a mysteriously long session of fleeting seconds. It was his wife. How the hell was she there? Which stupid guy had the nerve to call her here? As Adarsh moved forward she ran towards him. They held each other in a swift short embrace. She was trying hard to fight back her tears. Her eyes were a swollen red. Adarsh bit his lips, gave her a strong reassuring hug with his right hand and just walked through the door and entered the dimly lit court room to face the inevitable.

The magistrate though robed in royal black flowing legal gowns sat huddled like a plump nervous cat in his high-backed chair, behind heaps of dusty dog-eared case records piled up on both sides of his large table. His face was red and sweaty from the stuffy humid atmosphere inside the room.

Adarsh glanced behind. He could see the small figure of his wife trying to push her way in through the crowd. He took a deep breath and stifled the emotion welling up within. There was an impending threat staring right down his face. He must deal with that first. Other things could be taken care of later.

Without giving any breather, the public prosecutor blurted out in full flow about the serious nature of charges leveled against the accused, playing to the gallery with dramatic gestures pointing a long finger at Adarsh, to the cheers and shouts of the mob. Adarsh closed his eyes tight and took a very deep breath in silent meditation, calming his own emotions, trying to capture his inner strength, not allowing any random thought to dislodge the self within. That is what they had taught him at school for facing the audience as the curtains rolled up before a dramatic show. Later, he had also learnt at the university that a tragic hero when confronted with challenge, be it physical or psychological, had to take a decision all on his own. There was no one else in the world who could help or advise him at that critical juncture. It was just he and the moment. There was nothing else between them.

As the judge fidgeted in his seat and was taking up the pen to hurriedly write his order, Adarsh opened his eyes and firmly stated that he wanted to make a statement which should be recorded. He did not know why he said that. But something within him prompted that there was a definite need for his side of the story to be heard. They couldn't just shut his mouth and go on heaping all sorts of wild allegations against him, setting him up as a downright culprit.

But the timid judge just couldn't pick up enough courage to allow him to speak in the face of the clamoring crowd. He said there was no need of that just now. "Why? Why are you not allowing him to speak? He has every right to do so", a shrill woman's voice broke through the general din in the court room. Adarsh looked back. It was his wife. From among the hundreds of people gathered there, she alone had the courage to take them on all alone, asking for justice. The whole court room fell silent. The judge gestured towards her to come forward. Her face was flushed red with indignation. "Sir," she went on, unacquainted with the complicated procedures and decorum of the court room. "Why is it that my husband has been arrested this way and brought before you as a criminal? What crime has he committed?" Neither the judge, nor the lawyers had any answer to that downright simple question. They all looked stunned and were at a loss for answer. Only the crowd continued with their thoughtless shouting outside. After some moments of uneasy silence, the public prosecutor came up with a clumsy retort. "If your husband is innocent why are all these people shouting outside?" "They are shouting because they are all ignorant. They are half-starved and vulnerable immigrants whom you have influenced and misled into thinking that my husband is a culprit. My husband has been neglecting his family and slogging day in and out, risking his very life to save theirs and bring them relief from disaster, and you have now all ganged up against him and turned them all against him to settle your personal political score."

Her words, though infallible to the last syllable, could not cut much ice with the powers that be. She just looked on helplessly at the judge who did not speak a word as they huddled Adarsh onto a waiting jeep and sped away headed for the district jail. Adarsh looked back to have a last parting glimpse of her, but she was soon lost among the milling crowd.

The jailor was at his desk doing his routine job which he did every day. He was registering the particulars of the new prisoners, their names and addresses and the sections under which they had been apprehended. The assistant jailor was helping him depositing the rings and other valuables taken off the necks and fingers of the prisoners and giving them a number before sending them off into the foreboding enclave which lay beyond the iron gates. Adarsh too stood in line with some twenty other ill-fated ones for his turn to come. The jailor did not look up from his work as the papers were thrust before him. He went over the sections and mumbled "Theft, Abetment, Criminal Conspiracy....." each word hitting the core of Adarsh's soul. Suddenly seeing the name the jailor looked up in shock. His eyes met Adarsh's and stood fixed for a moment. Just a week back Adarsh had been the acting Jail Superintendent. It was a normal practice to depute Executive Magistrates to officiate whenever any regular important officer happened to be on leave. The jailor was a good man. He quickly got up and pulled in a chair asking Adarsh to sit. Adarsh thanked him and preferred to stand. He wanted to go through the entire experience of a new prisoner. Perhaps it would give him a better insight about how it felt being on the other side of the law, for a change. He quietly took off his wedding ring and the gold chain which his mother had given him on a birthday and the wrist watch, gifted recently by his wife, and deposited them with the assistant jailor, like everyone else. The jailor was immensely apologetic and took the trouble to accompany him himself to the waiting empty prison room. It was not a regular barred cell, but a separate one room tin-roofed house with a single door and window on the same side. There was a narrow bed with a thin mattress and a pillow and mosquito net in one corner with a rough brown blanket on it. A single bulb hung down from a long wire from the roof and there was a small ceiling fan beside. The jailor said that he would be sending in the dinner although it was past 5:00 pm. All the other prisoners had had their food and were now all locked up in their respective cells. There was a look of benignity in his eyes when he went on to say that he would be sending the meal from the hospital quota, which was better than the regular stuff which they served the other prisoners, because it contained a fish or egg curry. "This is all I can do Sir, you know my limits. I am really sorry for what has happened Sir." Adarsh patted him on the shoulder, "Thank you so much for the kindness. I'll be fine. Good night." He watched the jailor go out and heard the click of the lock as he shut the door behind him. An abyss of loneliness suddenly descended upon the room and Adarsh walked slowly towards the open window. All he could see outside was sheer desolateness. A pale frail light of a bulb burning somewhere, was struggling hard to keep the monstrous darkness, hovering menacingly around, at bay.

The prison blanket was very rough. Adarsh pulled it, all the same, over him and lay motionless, gazing emptily at the ceiling. But everything was blank in front of his eyes. The series of supports on which he had banked had all caved in one by one over the last two days. Things had moved so fast that he had no time to have a grasp of anything. Now everything had slipped out of his hand and he had hit the nadir of existence. He closed his eyes and tried to think. But all he could see was darkness. It looked as if he had lost the very power of thinking. Like his friends and colleagues even ideas had all deserted him.

He did not know for how long he had been lying that way when there was a creaking sound of the lock opening, a sharp sound of the latch being pulled and the door was thrown open. Five disheveled hefty looking men, with blankets wrapped around, were shoved into his room like animals by the jailor, and ordered to sit in line on the floor on the far side from his bed, with their back against the wall. Before Adarsh could react, the jailor explained that they would be there with him in the room during the night time every day. This was because the orders were that Adarsh should not be kept in solitary confinement. It was the practice, as Adarsh later came to know, not to keep any under-trial prisoner, especially the educated ones, all alone, in order to prevent him or her from resorting to any extreme steps like suicide etc. The jailor briskly wished goodnight and left.

Adarsh looked at the row of grim faces lined up in front of him. But none of them were looking back at him. They sat there, motionless and silent, staring hard at the floor. He took his time to look them up one by one. This was a completely new experience for him; sitting with a gang of rough grim looking prisoners in a cold locked prison room. He was as much shocked as he was a tad afraid and apprehensive. Who knows what they would do. He imagined all sorts of gruesome acts which he had seen in movies, that long serving hardened prisoners might indulge in as they were wont with new inmates; murder, ragging, roughing up, sodomy et al.… But as the hours passed, he found them dozing off, sitting as they were. He took his time to look them up one by one. He studied their dark weather-beaten faces. Their sturdy body structure and arms and legs showed that they were all hard labourers; accustomed to plowing hard soil to turn it to gold with the sweat of their brow, pulling callous passengers along the rough pebbled roads of life on some rickety cycle rickshaw perhaps, or pushing heavy cartloads up some steep highway beyond the muddy pathways of some remote unknown village somewhere, or maybe carrying backbreaking loads of the world on their sturdy shoulders to eke out a living for their loved ones back home. One thing which was absolutely clear was that they were all poor people---the have-nots. Adarsh wondered what thoughts were at this time passing through their minds. Or were they finished with all those thinking and were just tired and now just wanted to rest. He wondered what sort of crime they might have committed or were accused of, which had landed them in this hell on earth. He wondered what their families were having to cope with to fill the yawning economic and traumatic gap after the head of the family had left. Sitting and dozing in a row against the wall before him, they looked so innocent and helpless. He felt like talking to them and to hear the long untold stories they each sure had to tell before they hardened and died within the cockles of the heart. Strangely, in spite of himself, he felt a bizarre sense of joy to have the opportunity to, at least, sit so close to these few specimens of the millions of faceless masses that make the world go on; to nurture and feed the privileged few with their toil and sweat. The squeaky illiterate voice of the frail professional bailer came on resounding in his mind. Just after the court was over one day, and all had dispersed, this lean guy had lingered on in the chamber. He had come hesitatingly near the Magistrate's Chair of Adarsh and asked if he could have a word with him. A demonic air of superiority inexplicably hangs around the post of authority one occupies; the higher the post, the higher the air. So, at first, Adarsh was naturally taken aback by this impudent audacity. But on second thoughts, when he had successfully dispelled the air of authority and come down to earth, he called him over and smilingly asked the guy what he had to say. "Sir, please don't mind", he began, "but do you know why you are sitting on that Chair today?" Before Adarsh could gasp for words, he continued, the words hitting the point loud and clear. "Sir no one except Allah, or the Almighty God, as you say, has the authority to judge anyone in this world. That He has given you the authority to judge people in this world by sitting on that Chair is because you must have done something good in your previous life. Sir, so always please remember this and do justice because Allah has given this power to you, a human being, to judge another human being like yourself." The disgraced Christ had uttered as much before the mighty Roman governor Pontius Pilate, two thousand years ago. Scores of scholarly books have been written since on the idea of Justice and Equity. But no Shakespeare, Hobbes, Rousseau, Voltaire, John Rawls or Amartya Sen could ever drive home the point with such precision and poignancy, as the squeaky feeble words of that insignificant looking professional bailer did to Adarsh that day.

That night Adarsh couldn't sleep. Tossing and turning within the coarse blankets, he kept on thinking what to do. Every door was shut upon him. His boss, the Deputy Commissioner, whom he adored, had just let him slip out of his protection into the general atmosphere of political hostility raging all around him. His friends had been advised to cut off all communication with him. Even the local bar council had resolved to boycott him. The judge, yes the judge who was there to dispense justice, succumbing to organized public agitation and media propaganda had not allowed him to make a statement as envisaged under the law, but had rejected his application for bail outright, without even allowing him to speak a word. Adarsh involuntarily rose and sat up on his bed engulfed with darkness all around. As he was sitting there all blanked out a sudden thought came to his mind. He had no idea whatsoever how or wherefrom it sprung. In that dark lonely prison room all forsaken and abandoned, where he could not see any light, the words of the Mahatma Gandhi came to him in a soft unheard whisper. *When all roads are closed to you, look within and you will find the light.* Yes! He did exactly that and a blaring truth dawned upon him at once. He suddenly remembered that it was he who had first reported about the missing truck to the police at 2:00 am in the night. It was on the basis of his First Information Report that the investigation had started in the very night itself. The subsequent FIR filed by the Member of Parliament and his lackeys against him, was submitted sometime around 10:30 am to 11:00 am in the forenoon that day. It was on this second FIR that the judge had acted upon, and his bail rejected. No one, including himself had thought of this and brought it to the notice of the judge when he was produced in the court in the afternoon. But being a magistrate himself he had not cared to put his FIR down in writing and, therefore, there was no record of the same among the papers furnished before the court. Adarsh became immensely restless. He felt like as if to run out and inform everyone about it there and then, and proclaim it from the rooftops. But it was now again 2 O'clock in the night. There was no police, no lawyer, and no court to listen to him. He had to wait till the morning to do anything about it. It was a restless and endless waiting; a wait that seemed eternal.

With the dawn came more ideas. There was Mr Barooah, the retired Government Pleader. He was an upright and bold advocate who did not care much about political opinion and public propaganda and didn't mince words to call a spade a spade. Somehow in the course of official work, Adarsh and he had become quiet friendly. It was a friendship built upon mutual respect. Adarsh was certain that he had found his man. If there was anyone who would understand his viewpoint and dare take up his case in that hostile atmosphere, it had to be Mr Barooah and no one else. He was sure that Mr Barooah would not let him down. In spite of his advanced age he still had the fire in his guts to take on the toughest of challenges. He had seen him doing so during the Students' Movement, when the police had tried to beat up some unarmed protesters when they had defied the curfew. He must get word to him to come and meet him in the prison somehow….But how?

As breakfast was being served, Adarsh came up to the window of his cell. He could see the Assistant Jailor standing at some distance, passing instructions to some of the prison inmates who had lined up in front of him. He waved to him frantically. But he was looking elsewhere and did not notice. Adarsh was now desperate. If anything had to be done it had to be done during the court working hours. Else he had to wait for another full day. And what a torturous wait it would be. Without caring for consequences, Adarsh opened the door and came out into the open. An orderly saw him do so and came rushing towards him. Adarsh gestured to him that he wanted to say something to him for just a moment. He told the orderly to tell the Assistant Jailor that he wanted to speak to him urgently. The orderly was hesitant at first, but then he went and spoke to the Assistant Jailor. The Assistant Jailor looked towards Adarsh and gestured to him to wait for some time. Again the wait was endless. But he could finally manage to tell him what he wanted to.

Mr Barooah came at 11:32 am. Adarsh was escorted from his cell to the office of the Superintendent. Mr Barooah smiled and stretched out his hand magnanimously and they shook hands; a silent reassuring handshake which transcended words or oration. Mr Barooah knew his job. If Adarsh was the first to inform the police about the missing of the truck, it was the FIR which should have been taken cognizance of first. If not, both the FIRs should have been considered together. It was not fair to ignore the first FIR altogether and take cognizance of the second one only. In fact, the police had failed in their duty in not bringing out the fact of the first FIR, lodged by Adarsh at night, before the Hon'ble Court. But Adarsh had not submitted a written FIR, from where could they produce that? "No matter", said Mr Barooah, "whenever information of a crime is given to the police by someone, in written or verbally, it should be treated as an FIR, and recorded as such. In case they had not done so there is the Case Diary which every police station is to maintain. The information you had given should have been recorded in the Case Diary. We need to get a certified copy of that, and produce the same before the court, and make a fresh application for bail. Wait, I'll go and get the copy."

Misfortunes, they say, never come singly. Adarsh had hit the rock bottom, but his ordeal was far from over. Late in the afternoon, news came to him that his wife and other relatives had come to meet him. Adarsh hurried out of his room along with the escort and saw her there standing with her brother and his own brother-in-law. Her eyes were wet and they were looking at him. No words, just that distant look, which he had seen reflected in the swirling waters from the steamer, piercing through his very soul. "Her dad, your father-in-law is no more", the brother-in-law said. He passed away in the hospital yesterday". What was there left to say? What consolation would it bring? *Baban*, as they called him, was a gem of a person that Adarsh had ever met. His bearing, and the way he spoke, ever so mannerly, captured your soul the moment you saw him. Adarsh never remembered to have ever seen him angry or lose his composure. The grandchildren just adored him. Once a robust football player, he had transformed with age into a gentle soul. His soft smile said it all. He was vastly popular without making a sound. The way he moved around the house and went about his work would hardly make any one aware that he was around. But he was no sissy, and never hesitated to call a spade a spade. He corrected people when they were wrong, but did so ever so gently that no one could ever have nursed a grouse against him. He left as silently as he had lived. But such people leave behind an immense gulf of emotional attachment which is impossible to fill. But they also leave behind an assurance that wherever they be, they would make their surroundings placid and beautiful.

As he instinctively held her hand and took her in his embrace there was no words exchanged. Later he held her by the shoulder and muttered mechanically, "Don't worry, we're all there. All will be OK", acutely aware that, as of now, nothing was OK. The irony of a hopeless person, sunk neck-deep in trouble giving hope to someone, was not lost, either on him or the others who were standing by. Then they dispersed bidding silent goodbyes and assurances. Everyone's eyes were moist but Adarsh had no time to indulge in such sentimentalities just then. He had turned his heart to stone, plucked out the cutout, as if, from the switch board of the mind, to arrest the flow of any current of emotion, lest they become a hindrance to the pressing job at hand.

The long impatient night was consoled with a frail last ray of hope. As the eagerly awaited dawn broke ever so slowly, Adarsh got up from his bed, had a quick bath with half the bucket of cold water which remained after use for the lavatory. He put on his sole pair of jeans and white T-shirt that was carefully hung on a rusty nail on the wall beside his bed. He went to the open window and pressed his face against the iron rods, his hands involuntary clasping them and ineffectively pushing to break through. The long rectangular courtyard where they lined up the prisoners every morning and evening was empty and desolate, eagerly awaiting the trample of depressing footsteps of scores of wretched unwilling feet, which lined up there every morning and evening for roll call. The all-pervading Wait which equally permeated both the animate and the inanimate, engendering Hope--- the vacant sky for the clouds, the parched Earth for the rain, the lover for the beloved, the blind beggar for that tinkle of a coin in his empty battered bowl, the hungry forest prowlers for the night, the unemployed for the call letter, the patient for the doctor, the prisoner for the bail.

It was exactly 9:30 when Advocate Barooah arrived. Adarsh was ushered from his cell and led to the office of the Jail Superintendent. Mr Barooah had obtained the certified copy of the Diary Entry from the police station and had the bail petition typed and ready. All Adarsh had to do was to put a signature on it vertically along the right edge of the pages and on the *waqaltnama*, authorizing Advocate Barooah to plead his case. But there was a problem which had to be sorted out first. They needed a bailer. The person required to have his land documents ready at hand. The title over the land has to be clear and authentic, the land unencumbered from any mortgage etc., and the revenue tax paid up to date. Now, where to get such a person; all on a sudden, and so soon? So many friends, so many relatives, but not one was coming to the mind of Adarsh, who had that entire ready requirement. Besides, where was the time to confirm from each of them about each of these requisites? It would take at least a week if not a fortnight or more at the earliest. The Assistant Jailor, who had been witnessing all the conversation from a distance, now came forward and whispered something to Mr Barooah. He suggested that they get hold of a professional bailer by paying him something. There were quite a few of them always loitering around the court premises. This was their business. Adarsh was instinctively revolted by the very idea and asked how could that be. The Assistant Jailor's face turned serious. "See, I've suggested a way out of your predicament. Now it is up to you to decide whether to accept it or not." Saying so he just turned and left, indicating that he had other important things to do. In the face of the grave circumstance at hand Adarsh had finally to give in. He knew he was innocent, but still he was in prison. He had to prove to the world that he was innocent. There was still a long battle ahead of him. How could he fight a battle if he was down in a ditch? He needed to come out of it first.

That night Adarsh had an uneasy sleep, if sleep it could be called. Confused images and faces, some known some unknown kept coming and going in a bizarre collage with jumbled thoughts till the cawing of the crow announced the break of dawn.

Advocate Barooah came sharp at ten along with the prospective bailer. He was the same very guy who had told Adarsh about the responsibilities of a judge, that it was a gift of God. No one, but God had the right to judge anyone, it is only those who had done something good in their previous life who were given the privilege to do so on this earth. Adarsh looked at the skinny bailer and wondered what philosophy he would have to expound now when the judge himself was in jail. But the thoughts remained unspoken and they came down straight to business. The deal was finally closed at five thousand rupees. Adarsh had no money with him but his relatives would be there by 12 noon and pay the bailer his fees. Advocate Barooah undertook to stand guarantee and so the papers were readied and signed. They would move the bail at 11 O'clock when the judge would ascend his judgment seat. A quick mixed look of hope and despair was exchanged and they left for the Court and Adarsh habitually turned and headed back to his cell for the last final wait.

The day was getting warmer by the minute. The rusty ceiling fan was rumbling monotonously as it turned and turned. Adarsh looked at it and wondered for how many donkeys' years it had been doing so. Going round and round for so long to no end, it had lost its early gust and vigor. It went on slow and painfully doing the rounds in a routine manner, and would go on doing so, bereft of any feeling of hope or change till it would finally come to a grinding halt on its own. Adarsh knew that the monotonous grinding sound of that slow revolving fan would always be subconsciously ringing in his ears for the rest of his life. It had entered the core of his soul. The grinding sound, the changeless movement, that absolute lack of speed, dash and hurry --- all of this would dictate his future course of life, be it in prison or outside. Because even if he were to get his bail and be free once again, that forlorn and empty cell would forever be imprisoned within his soul.

Adarsh was unmoved when they all came in at around 2:30 in the afternoon to announce that he had been extremely lucky. The Court had granted him the bail. As they stuffed his few belongings into the knapsack which was lying all this while in one corner of the cell and the jailor handed over the purse and the gold ring which they had taken away when they had brought him in there, Adarsh thought of the many unfortunate ones whom he was leaving behind in jail which had been his house address too for a time. He thought of the so many families in far away villages and towns who were going about their lusterless daily chores missing one of their dear ones, as if dead though not dead, gone away to some distant land, abandoning them to their fate. He thought of crimes and why they were committed, the circumstances which lead to the breakdown point and of that fateful scrap of time which changed everything forever. He thought of the so many criminals who were at large and the few so called hapless ones who were hemmed in there, sometimes so very wrongly.

As the car sped away on the road leaving a nightmare behind, Adarsh looked out the window and allowed the strong wind to hit him straight in the face. It was fresh air he was breathing --- the open air under a bright and mellow sunshine. He popped his head out and looked askance at the wide open clear blue sky. He looked at the tall trees passing him by and the lush green grass and the shady undergrowth beneath. They had always been there as they were, free and ungrudging in showering their bounty upon the world and all its inmates, but he had had no time to stop and ever take notice, as he had so many other, so called, important and pressing things to attend to.

As the car took the sharp bend and landed onto the highway he saw the mighty river Bramhaputra come into full view alongside. Its deep and dark blue waters were absolutely calm forming graceful ripples that sparkled under the blazing sun. It flowed along silent and majestically by, innocent of any turmoil, angst or fury whatsoever. Totally oblivious of any calamitous havoc that it could wreak.

GLOSSARY

bandhs	– Total Closure of business and traffic in protest
dada	– a Hector, a bully
dhaba	– highway tavern
Digamber	– saintly people who wear no clothes as a sign of renunciation
Durga Mai Ki Jai	– All Hail to Mother Durga
Lakshman-rekha	– line of limit
mama	– maternal uncle
Sindur	– vermillion
SITREP	– law & order situation report
tamul-pan	– betel nut and betel leaf chewed with a dash of white lime